# WHEN THE MOUNTAINS CALLED

### Shannon Baker

# SOLUM
## LITERARY PRESS

Scottsdale, AZ • solumpress.com

# WHEN THE
# MOUNTAINS CALLED

A crumbling fence. Fireflies beyond a cracked window. The burning house. I seldom cry over a book, but Tacito's reluctant quest intrigued, then disarmed, my heart. Come, smell the sacred obsidian fire stoked by laughter; witness the mystical, midriver girl in her swirl of black skirts. Eavesdrop on burly Macario, wise and unlikely guide: "Words resurrect the dead. . . . And stories give them a place to stay." I loved this tale of unearthing, told with the cadence of myth, the pearlescence of truth. O how our "words matter—when [we dare] to share them."

—LAURIE KLEIN, author of *House of 49 Doors: Entries in a Life*

Baker weaves a lovely and elegiac mystery that takes the reader by the hand and leads them with skill and confidence through the darkest paths of the grieving human heart to glimpse what lies beyond.

—MIKE BONIKOWSKY, author of *The Shepherd of Princes*

Shannon Baker's *When the Mountains Called* pulls you in like an afternoon daydream, with each page a rock overturned and a galaxy lurking underneath. Losing Pearl, greater than anything—including his own life—thrusts Andrew into a figurative death where he chokes out any remembrance of his wife. But the mountains call, so Andrew follows. Soon, you discover your journey paralleling Andrew's.

As you trek through grief's valley, plateau, and mountaintop, you discover a surprising balm for the sorrowful heart: "*Words resurrect.*" During Andrew's journey, you learn storytelling's profound vitality for the grief-stricken, revealing the heart's capacity to hold grief and gratefulness in tandem. Though gone from the living, Pearl teaches Andrew how to live and honor those dear, showing that the stories we live, remember, and share with others truly heal.

This is a must-read-in-one-sitting book, for the mountains do not call just to Andrew—the mountains are calling you, too.

—MEGAN HUWA, author and editor

Deep allegory, artfully unwrapped. A healing discovery. *When the Mountains Called* is both intriguing and enchanting. Shannon invites us to revivify wonder long lost and to engage with life purposefully. Richly colorful and insightful, this contemplative novella empowers our return to a fresh and joyful life well lived.
—CURT LINVILLE, author, entrepreneur, amateur philosopher

Author Shannon Baker invites her readers on an unforgettable journey, brilliantly and on the edge of poetically connecting the dots and blurring the lines between a glorious and magical vision of the afterlife with a very real and heartfelt quest for healing from grief. . . and for hope. The river is safe, and this skillfully crafted and inspired story will sing to your soul.
—MIKE HOUSHOLDER, Senior Pastor of Lutheran Church of Hope

A talented writer and storyteller, Shannon has a gift for words and creating visual imagery. In that light, *When the Mountains Called* is a haunting and spiritual tale that draws you in as you accompany the main character on a thought-provoking journey filled with grief, discovery, understanding and, eventually, healing.
—MARK YONTZ, communications professional, author & ghostwriter

Solum Literary Press
15850 N Thompson Peak Pkwy, 2176
Scottsdale, AZ 85260

solumpress.com

PAPERBACK ISBN 978-1-965169-00-1
EBOOK ISBN 978-1-965169-01-8

Cover art and design by Sarah Christolini.
Illustrations by Sarah Christolini.
Interior design by Riley Bounds and Sarah Christolini.
Author photo by Sarah Ellen. Used with permission.

---

LIBRARY OF CONGRESS CATALOGUING-IN-PUBLICATION DATA
Name: Baker, Shannon, author.
Title: When the mountains called / shannon baker.
Description: Scottsdale, AZ: Solum Literary Press, 2024.
Identifiers: LCCN 2024942694
ISBN: 978-1-965169-00-1 (print)
ISBN 978-1-965169-01-8 (ePub)
Subjects: BISAC: YOUNG ADULT FICTION / Literary | Religious / Christian / Fantasy | Social Themes / Death, Grief, and Bereavement
LC record available at https://lccn.loc.gov/2024942694

For the Yarrows, and for all who seek peace in the Valley.

# CONTENTS

*Acknowledgments* | x

Chapter 1 | 1
Chapter 2 | 5
Chapter 3 | 11
Chapter 4 | 17
Chapter 5 | 25
Chapter 6 | 37
Chapter 7 | 48
Chapter 8 | 59
Chapter 9 | 76
Chapter 10 | 87

## Acknowledgments

First and foremost, a massive thank you to Riley Bounds, Christine Pelliccio, and the rest of the Solum Editorial Team for believing in this story and for getting it out into the world. You have made a childhood dream a reality (and this adult writer's heart very happy).

To Mom, Dad, Sarah, and Jackson—thank you for reading my stories and reminding me of my gifts. You are the best supporters I could ask for, and I thank God every single day for you.

To Dr. Amy Weldon—thank you for helping me hone my story-telling craft and encouraging me to share it with the world. You are an inspiration and a light, and the world could use more teachers like you.

To Caleb and Curt—thank you for your creative insight, partnership, and cheerleading, and for making space for Andrew to journey in the first place.

To Jeff, Ann, Ross, Dayton, and Josh—thank you for teaching me how to climb mountains and how to sit in the Valley. You are stronger than you know.

To all my friends and family who read this story in its unpublished days, thank you for being people I can trust. No matter how long it's been, you're welcome to come walk in the woods and gather syrup anytime.

Finally, last but never least, thank you, Jesus, my companion and my friend, my Macario forever, for leading me into the mountains and beyond, and for calling me in the first place. You are the reason for it all.

# WHEN THE MOUNTAINS CALLED

# Chapter 1

When the mountains first called to him, he was in the valley, and more importantly, he was alive.

It had been sunset. The horizon was golden, like the dried turnips he'd shelved earlier that day, the dulling sun pink and low, a cupped egg cradled by the hands of the darkening sky on either side. In the field where he stood, the grass blew against his ankles, scraping the bottoms of the tattering corduroy pants he'd always worn because they were simple and good and all he'd known.

All he'd known, all he'd known, like the path he'd walked from his small cabin this night as he had every other night, to stand at the lowest part of the valley but never beyond. Like the rolling hills that rippled from beyond the crumbling wooden fence he had put up years before, not so much to keep others out as to keep himself in. Because this path, these hills, the cabin, was simple and good, simple and good, and all he'd known.

Comfortable, how comfortable, to be alone. How comfortable, like the sun, like that cradled egg, cupped and held and carried always by the routine-ridden sky around it. How comfortable, comfortable, only rough when he thought about it, only itchy when he noticed it, like the corduroy pants whose scratchy interiors had at first rubbed his calves raw by overuse but had since become commonplace and warm. Now, it itched to take them off. So, he didn't. When the mountains first called to him, it was nothing he'd known, and for that reason, he'd ignored them. He ignored their soft whispers that rode on the wind, the ones that ruffled the grasses so that his corduroy pants moved and itched his legs again for the first time in twenty-five years. He ignored the new smell that wafted on the breeze, something like goldenrod, or maybe the gold of the sun itself—the one that he stared at—willing his nostrils to close against the whisk of the wind. He stared at the lowest point of the valley that outlined the base of the stolid mountains rising above, the ones whose purple rock he ignored, so fixated was he on the running groove of the valley and the comfortable boundary it created.

Comfortable, how comfortable, to maintain that barrier between valley and mountain, between river and hill, between what was good and simple and what was harsh and complicated, between the certainty of life and—the only thing he could see in the rare moments he chose to look at the deepening, jagged mountains that stabbed his soft, pink sky—the fragility of death.

This was here: his field, his house, his self-sustaining way of life that called for no one and nothing else as long as they both should live; and that was beyond: the place past the hills and the river, the mountains, and whatever lay within them.

When the mountains first called to him, he was in the valley, and he was alive. He did not pay them attention, but that did not mean that he did not hear, as much as he tried not to. Come, come, they said, but he would not, he would not, because he had no need to. He was comfortable, and it would be great risk to leave. Great risk, and for what reward? What did the mountains have that he did not?

There in the field, in the spreading twilight, alive, he closed his eyes and crouched down to still his rustling trousers against the dampening grass, pressing his hands to his ears to drown out the beckoning wind. Above him, the hands of the sky released the egg that they held until it sunk lower and lower, finally cracking against the horizon, spilling its dull light so thin against the earth that its glow was soon swallowed up and he was left in the dark and the still of the night. Quiet, quiet. Simple and quiet, and all he'd known.

The next time the mountains called to him, he was no longer in the valley, and he was dead.

\*\*\*

He didn't know he was dead at first, but he figured it out soon enough, when he couldn't get back to the house and cellar that had been his whole life. He tried to get back—to cross that falling-down fence and return to the blowing grasses that felt different than the ones by the river because they were his—but he couldn't. Something prevented him. He willed every muscle in his body to propel his leg forward over the lowest, most crumbled part of the fence and into his field where the two dappled horses—the ones that Pearl kept—used to graze. But he could not move. He could not lift even a foot past the fence. It was as if an invisible wall extended from the rotting posts straight upward to the sky, around the entire perimeter of his property where the fence ran, a fact he found out as he jogged the boundary, stopping every few yards to try to cross. But each time he tried, his legs felt heavy, as if they had been wrapped in taffy, and he would put them back down, feel the taffy loosen, and run again.

He was exhausted by the time he reached that first part of the fence again, the one that, earlier, he'd so easily crossed to get where he was now trapped. His breath came out in short, strangled gasps, deafeningly loud in the now-windless air. He could feel the mallet of his heart in his chest, straining partly from fatigue and partly from terror. Only one time before had he felt this way—equal parts tired and terrified—but he didn't want to think about that now. Now, he had nothing left to do but sit. Sit and ho. . . no. None of that, that would get nowhere. He would only wait. Wait for the normalcy to return, because in the last twenty-five years, he had found normalcy, or normalcy had found him—*saved* him—and it would save him again. He just had to wait.

So, he sat down, just outside the fence, a quarter mile from his small house, and waited, waited for that thing that had saved him before to come again. It would. It had to. If it didn't, he didn't know what he would do.

But eventually—he didn't know how long—something else came. A sound—that sound. *Come*, it said. *Come*. It was gentle, but it was insistent, and his tired, terrified heart tugged towards the distant snow-covered peaks. *No*, he whispered to himself. *No*.

It had been twenty-five years since he had journeyed from the town he and Pearl had lived in, the one just twenty miles away, now also forbidden by the invisible barrier that separated him from his house, the house that, for thirty years had been their little ranch cabin but had since become his permanent refuge. Away from the town, away from memories of her and the life they had had, away from those disappeared evening walks and porch-side dinners and slow mornings with coffee and the paper and Pearl humming as she baked. Just away, and that became comfortable. Just far enough, and no further, far enough to not be within sight of the town, near enough to yet in some way be tethered to her. It was still painful, and maybe would always be painful, he realized, but at some point, he had gotten used to the pain, just like he had gotten used to the corduroy pants that tickled his ankles in this foreign breeze.

When Pearl died, a part of him had died with her. But he had accepted that, he had become OK with that, saved by the comfort of the little ranch cabin. He had sold the horses immediately—they reminded him too much of Pearl—but he had kept the cabin and the fields and the gardens they'd tended as a team, because giving those up felt too much like betrayal, a gut-wrenching disposal of the last thing they had built together.

But the half-tired, half-terrified feeling was back, acid pumping in his heart, and with a weathered hand to his chest, he closed his eyes. The feeling he had felt twenty-five years ago— sharp at first but that had, over time, dulled to nothingness—was back. It was back, and it was strong, and he couldn't return to his house. That, and the mountains were calling. The mountains were calling and he could not go home. Life had been quiet and comfortable, and this, therefore, this new thing, could not be life.

For all intents and purposes, he was dead, and still the mountains called.

# Chapter 2

*The river is safe.*

*Float on through, do not fear. Its water is strong and steady, and it is stronger than you, but do not be afraid. Its strength is for you, and it will carry you, past all your memories that wait on the banks, that loom from the banks, over your head to catch you and snag you and keep you from flowing past as you are made to do, if you only let go.*

*Let go. The river is safe.*

*Your memories wait on the banks—the ones that are good and the ones that are bad—waiting, just waiting, for you to float past and see them and be reminded of things you thought were dead and gone. And when you do, when you relax into the current and are carried by these memories, you will cringe as you pass the bad ones, the ones that are pain and sadness and loss. But it's often the good ones that hurt the most: the ones of joy and peace and sepia-covered better days, the ones that hurt because they are what they are now: just memories.*

*When you pass the memories, it's tempting to turn against the current and swim upstream—or try to—to get away from the bad ones, or to frantically chase after the good ones, those painful past joys that tug at your heart and tell you that it's life back there. But swimming against the current is tiring, and it only prolongs your exposure to the good and bad memories, both of which can hurt you if you're not careful, because they're on the banks now, and, by their nature, are meant to be observed but not lived.*

*Do not swim against the current. It is fruitless, and exhausting, and if you only would surrender to its path, the current will carry you along, past the painful memories—good and bad—no matter how many times it has had to do so before. For you will pass them—these memories—the ones on the banks. You will observe them and be reminded of them, but do not be afraid—they cannot hurt you—and do not be ashamed. It is life to remember these things, to remember the pain and joy, but it is not life to dwell in them. The river knows this, and it wants to help you.*

*Take a deep breath, and float. You might pass the memories thousands of times in this particular loop of the river, and yet, though you do not, the current knows its path and knows the way out. Do not fight the current. Do not cling to the banks. Loosen your fingertips and let the blood flow to your knuckles again, the ones that have clung so long to a bank that offers nothing but sore joints and the pretense of life, and let go.*

*The river is safe. It will cradle you; it will carry you, and you do not have to be afraid. Right now, you fix your eyes on what it seeks to carry you from, and not the life it promises to carry you towards. Instead, look forward: The current is constant; the promise is there.*

*But it is your choice to trust it.*

\*\*\*

He woke up across the river at the bottom of the valley, curled on the grass that blew at the foothills of the mountains.

It had been a dream, but the pain he felt in his gut when he woke up confused him, blurring the line between dreamland and reality. Though, of course, he knew, he was for-all-intents-and-purposes *dead*, and so perhaps it hadn't been a dream at all—the image of the river, floating by the memories on the banks, the call to let the current carry him, the painful tug he felt in his gut in trying to do so. Perhaps, now that he was dead, dreams and reality weren't so easily separable. He could no longer simply wake up, push the dream away, and leave his little shack of a house to pull up carrots in the garden or stare out at the boundary of the valley below his fields. He could not make just one cup of coffee, ignoring Pearl's cracked, dusty, peach-colored mug that hung from the iron hooks that had also claimed her cookware for the past twenty-five years. He could not sit on the porch, watching the ants investigate the particularly mossy floorboard on the second step, *which needed repairing,* he would think absentmindedly as he sipped his bitter cup, though of course he never would, because the rotting wood had become commonplace and comfortable and therefore had its place there in his home.

No, he could do none of these things, because he had somehow passed the boundary between his house and beyond, between what was considered life and what therefore had to only be death.

He lay on the grass at the base of the hills, just past the gentle swirling water of the river. He didn't remember swimming across, not even in his "dream," but somehow he was on the other side of the water, one step further from the home he hadn't left since Pearl had died. Perhaps that was why he felt such an ache in his stomach.

That, and he was hungry, which was frustrating, since he didn't think he, being dead, was supposed to be hungry. What could he eat out here? He had no pack, no water bottle—he was not at all prepared to hike and hunt for food, since he hadn't been hiking since the day before. . . no. He wouldn't think about it.

*Take a deep breath, and float,* said a voice in his mind, quoting his dream. *Don't swim away from the memories. Relax.*

He shook his head, as if that would shake the voice loose and cast it away into the soft breeze that swirled over the surface of the river beside him, forming eddies in the water.

He had been swimming away from memories for twenty-five years, turning his head from the banks the moment Pearl's soft blue eyes blinked into his mind. To not look, to not acknowledge, was to move on. And that is what he had done. He had *moved on*, pressing the memories to the banks of his mind, thinking that if he didn't— if he didn't push them as hard as he could—they would spill over the banks and into the river with him, swirling around his ankles and washing over his head, eventually pushing him under, *holding* him under, until he drowned in a baptism of the past.

His stomach tugged at him again. Did he really think that? Were his memories that malicious? He thought of Pearl, her soft laugh, her tough hands—weathered from gardening—which were still somehow the gentlest things he had ever felt when she held his wrist and leaned into him to watch the sun set below the peaks of the mountains. Surely any memory of her could not be so dangerous, so lethal, as to drown him if he looked at them. After all, he was already dead, wasn't he? Hadn't he already crossed that boundary?

His toe was in the river. He was hungry, but his toe was in the river. The water was cool, and it eased the tug in his stomach. He put his whole foot in. The bottoms of his corduroy pants instantly fanned out in the water, little pieces of sediment catching in the cuffs.

He looked up at the silhouette of his house in the distance where it stood on the hill, as it always had. If he got in the river, he would be leaving it.

*Do not cling to the banks.*

Would he be able to find his way back home? He wasn't sure. He didn't know what death allowed and what it did not. But he did know the way of the river, which he had watched for the past couple of decades from his fields. He knew that it meandered east, to the rising sun, and disappeared around the rolling hills, towards the base of the mountains beyond. Towards the mountains, which terrified him.

*The river is safe.*

He'd never been much of a swimmer, but then again, he was already dead. He waded in up to his hips, the iciness of the water shocking him and making his feet tingle. His pants filled with water, but the only tug he felt now was that of the current, insistent yet gentle.

*The current is constant; the promise is there.*

What promise? What was there to look to? Pearl was gone, and he was dead.

He looked up at his house. But if he was dead, then Pearl would be here, wouldn't she, traversing the hills, even floating in the river somewhere downstream, face angled up to the sun? He heart jolted at the thought. His gaze went downriver, towards the base of the mountains. *Come,* they had said. *Come.* To where? To her? His pulse quickened at the thought, his fingers tingled, and her blue eyes swam before him. Surely that was what they meant, surely that was why he was dead, to find her again?

Hope was dangerous. He'd learned that from the series of treatments. But he could not help but hope. It flickered in him, ignorant of the water around it, growing and growing.

He was up to his waist now. The current pulled, still gentle, still insistent.

*Let go. The river is safe.*

He looked back up at his house. If he let go, if he went with the river, he didn't know if he would ever be back. But he was dead, and the mountains called, and Pearl was out there somewhere. He was sure of it.

"Goodbye," he said softly, and let the current take him.

# Chapter 3

*Swish swish.*

His eyes fluttered against the tall, swaying grass of the river-bank, and he pressed them shut. The sun was warm upon his face, the water cool and rippling against his toes—which dangled in the water still—and he found himself thinking this wouldn't be such a bad place to stay awhile. He could nap perhaps, or truly, truly sleep, something he hadn't been very good at since Pearl had died.

*Pearl.* His eyes snapped open. The grass wasn't so soft anymore; its sharp yellow blades were actually rubbing quite uncomfortably against the whiskers on his cheeks. His feet were icy, and he retract-ed them to his chest, sitting upright on the bank. He looked to his left, upriver. He couldn't see anything but the field across the banks, yellow and rolling across the valley, and the river, sparkling, cold and clear, winding its way across it all until it disappeared around a corner—a pinprick in the distance. Had he really floated so far? He had no idea where he was; he had never been this way before. In all the hikes he had gone on with Pearl, all the day-expeditions in the early decades of their marriage—before she got sick—he wasn't sure he had ever been this far. The prairie grasses of the valley looked similar enough, but where he might have expected to see his little house on a hill in the distance, there was only the hypnotic sway of yellow—a never-ending field.

He didn't know how long he had floated in the river. At some point, he must have fallen asleep, and yet, he must have washed up on the banks long enough ago because—looking down he noticed—his clothes were already dry in the high heat of the day. Turning his head to the right, he eyed the river. About a mile away, it disap-peared around another corner, the yellow valley extending beyond the bank on the other side.

He weighed his options. He could ford the river, but then what? Meander aimlessly across the valley, forever surrounded by a golden sea? His house had to be to the left somewhere—that was where he had floated from—but he remembered the previous day (or days, however long ago it had been) when he had tried to return to his beloved house, his field, his garden. He remembered the invisible fence, and the futility of it all. No, it wouldn't profit him to wander across the valley.

He could keep floating, he thought. It had been peaceful enough, once he had made the decision to get in. And he had certainly been comfortable, wrapped and carried by the current. . .

He shook his head. This wasn't about him. This was about Pearl, about finding her. If they were both dead, then she was out there somewhere. But where?

He twisted his body where he sat on the bank, examining the surroundings behind him—it was pure woods—tall, ashen trunks, yellowing canopies interspersed with thick pines. And beyond that (he craned his neck up), in his direct line of vision, perhaps a few miles away—the clear blue of the sky was blotted out, interrupted instead by a block of solid grey rock that extended as far as he could see to the right and to the left. Tiny as toothpicks, the evergreen trees ran down it in gullies, as if they had been poured down from the sky, so numerous that they had spilled out to the forest floor below, planting themselves all the way to where he sat at the river. Above the treeline, however, was only the grey, ashy and solid, tinged with a deep purple above what he thought must be a ridgeline before the white-frosted summit. He sucked in his breath. He was nearly at the base of the mountains.

*Come, come,* they had said, and he had, without even really trying. All he had done was get in the river. Was this the reason he was stopped here, *here,* here at this bank, because they had called? Was he really so powerless in his direction? And if so, did he really believe he had a choice now? Did it *matter* what he wanted?

Had it mattered what Pearl had wanted? Had she finally had a choice, when, for the last several years of her life, she had only seemed to be able to let fate choose for her? He squeezed his eyes shut, trapping the tears within them. Blinking a few times, he opened them again.

Well. If Pearl had been here earlier, what would she have chosen? Would he find her if he floated downriver, or would it profit him to obey the call of the mountains? They were silent now, but they had brought him thus far.

He knew Pearl. He knew his wife. She, ever the adventurer, the one who had convinced him to move to the valley from town, who had spent the days outside, who had wrangled horses and planted gardens and who, on principle, only entered the little house once the sun had disappeared below the hills. Pearl, who had preferred only to rest at night, at least until the final years when her body had demanded otherwise. *This* Pearl—if death was redemptive at all, *this* first Pearl, the one of adventure and sun and endless day—was the one who had had to make this same choice on this same bank. And he knew what she would have chosen.

He grunted as he got to his feet, willing the achiness of his joints to dissipate so that he might be ready for the journey ahead. He had no pack, no food, no luggage, nor anything else, but that did not bother him. He was dead, after all, and the only thing he needed was to find his wife. That was why the mountains had called, to help him find her. And he would go to them.

*\*\*\**

The woods were denser than he had thought, as if no one had been there before. The tree roots twisted over one another, knotted and mossy so that his foot wedged between them, tripping him or, if he managed to step over them, caught the bottom of his boot in such a way that the slick green moss made him slip. Burrs lined his corduroy legs and every now and again poked through to his bare skin, pricking him. He found himself annoyed and vaguely disappointed, that pain as small as this was still present in death. Back when he had hoped, it had been for better. Still, he pushed on, driven by the steadily pulsing desire in his heart, the knowledge that Pearl was up in the mountains somewhere, waiting for him.

After hours—he didn't know how many, because as far as he could tell, the sun was still high in the sky—he took a break. He hadn't hiked like this in decades; in the years of Pearl's declining health, he had rarely left her side, and she hadn't been able to go much farther than the property line—the one now encased by an invisible fence. And when she had passed, she took the sense of adventure with her.

So, a break would do him good. His legs ached with overuse—also something he had hoped he might not have to deal with in death—and he was panting from the effort of climbing over downed trees and tree roots. Twenty yards to the right, he saw a large, blackened stump. He went to it and sat, heaving a sigh and closing his eyes. Opening them, he peered at the ground through his fingers, staring at his dirt-crusted boots, at the twigs caught in his laces. Pinching one, he pulled it from his laces and pressed the tip to the dirt floor. He got off the stump and, crouching in the dirt, began to write:

*Pearl, I went to the mountains. –A*

He stood and examined his work. It was legible enough, not the neatest, but then again, Pearl had always been able to read his hasty scrawl.

Of course, the odds of her seeing his note were quite slim. He was surrounded on either side by the thickest brush he had ever seen, and he was sure she was in the mountains already. Still, if she was here, in the woods, making her way to the mountains like him, then perhaps she would stumble upon this message scribbled in the dirt path.

The dirt path.

Heart pounding, he looked up. Extending in either direction beneath his mud-caked boots ran a winding path. Roots still ran across it, but it was unmistakably a path: branches were broken or sawn from the low-hanging trees above, and the dirt was packed in a way the rest of the forest was not. His eyes traced the path a few yards to the left, catching on something in the dirt. It was a faint semicircle just before a particularly large tree root, almost as if someone had pressed the ball of their foot to the root and their heel had dug into the ground behind them. His eyes skated forward. A few paces beyond was another print, clearly made by a boot.

His heartbeat quickened. He was not alone—someone else had

travelled this path, this path that might lead to the mountains, and they had done so fairly recently. He couldn't have been more than a mile away now from the base of the rocks, and this path would take him at least part of the way. It was better than bushwhacking, he decided.

He started out at a trot, his energy surging from somewhere deep inside, replenished by his quick rest and the fortune of his discovery. He kept his eyes to the ground, watching as the prints varied from half a heel to a whole foot, some of them facing forward and some of them turning back. They seemed to be created by the same person, but he couldn't know for sure. They weren't small enough to be Pearl's—this was a man's print—but that didn't mean that Pearl hadn't travelled this path at one point or another.

He ran into the evening, even as the sun cast a golden pall through the trees, whose shadows lengthened, whose needled branches refracted the light in such a way that it made his steps more concentrated so that he wouldn't stumble. The forest was flickering now, dizzying him, but still he pressed on, until it was twilight.

The forest was a deep green-grey, as if it had been covered by a translucent, silver blanket. Everything was soft, except the sharp outlines of the tree trunks—sentinels of the approaching night whose ranks still extended as far as he could see. He didn't want to be running at night, or searching for Pearl at night. Even in death, he could feel pain, and he could certainly feel cold, now quite evident in the absence of the sun. Were there still animals? He'd heard birds all throughout the day, so it wasn't impossible. It was best, then, to find shelter.

But where? All there were for miles were trees. He stepped off the path in search of a particularly big one with a wide base of thick-needled branches, beneath which he might be able to have some sort of covering. His eyes strained in dark. There, thirty yards to the left, maybe—

A rustle. Somewhere, behind him maybe, not far off. His hands turned to ice. His boots might as well have been filled with cement. The only things he heard were the thumping in his chest and the steadily increasing sound of pine branches being pushed aside. He couldn't move. He couldn't speak. If it was a large animal, he couldn't outrun it, not in the ever-blackening night, even with the safety of the path beneath his feet.

But. He took a deep breath. But, he reminded himself, he was already dead. He could not die twice, could he?

The rustle was closer now, louder, but now, he discerned, still frozen three feet off the path, it was accompanied by another sound, duller, tempered by something solid.

*Shhh*-crunch. *Shhh*-crunch.

Branches, whishing through the air. Footsteps, pressing against the ground.

He didn't move.

*Shhh*-crunch. *Shhh*-crunch.

Should he move? Thirty yards away, his shelter for the night.

*Shhh*-crunch. *Shhh*-crunch. Louder now.

*Shhhhhhhhhhhhh*-CRUNCH.

Then nothing.

He looked down the path, holding his breath. There, standing twenty yards away, just after the bend, just barely visible against the now deep-black woods beyond, was the outline of a man.

Perhaps the man wouldn't see him. If he stood very still—

"Mmmm." The man grunted, and the outline of his arm rose to remove a hat, holding it in the air before it swept back through the air and onto his head. The man's arm lifted again. Then, he spoke, his voice echoing through the night:

"Heavens bless, good. Finally. Here you are!"

# Chapter 4

The man's name was Macario, he said, but to everyone he knew well—which was apparently right after meeting them—it was just "Mac."

"Call me Mac," Macario—Mac—assured him. "And you are 'A.'" It wasn't a question. "But that's gotta be short for something?" This was a question.

"Andrew," he said, but then immediately wished he hadn't. He didn't know this man, however quickly he had learned his nickname.

As he came closer, Mac looked him up and down, his eyes fixating on Andrew's left hand, which was fidgeting at the seam of his now-torn corduroy pants. Mac stopped in front of him, staring with bright green eyes and a face that was almost timeless—certainly younger than himself, Andrew thought, whose own face was—now unshaven—whiskered white and running with grooved wrinkles from forehead to chin. On the other hand, Mac's eyes had only the crinkles formed from laughing, and though these were deep enough to suggest he did this recently and often, the rest of his face remained smooth and a deep tan. Closer now, even in the darkening night, Mac's body remained lit by the full moon rising overhead. Andrew studied his clothes—a backwoodsmen's clothes, he thought, with tan work pants and a red-and-black flannel—even these, though clearly worn, gave Andrew the feeling that they too were timeless, like Mac had worn them forever but hadn't needed to wash them once. It was a strange contradiction, but then again, everything was strange here. Death was strange, Andrew supposed, and he would leave it at that.

All this time, the men stood there, neither saying anything. Finally, Mac adjusted his wide-brim hat, hoisted a black, bulky pack on his shoulders, stepped around Andrew, and started off down the path. After a moment he turned. "Aren't you coming, Tacito?" he asked. Seeing Andrew's confusion, Mac laughed—a deep, resounding belly laugh, genuine, but enunciated: *Ha ha ha.* "Tacito," he said. "'Quiet one.' Though I guess 'Andrew' is fitting." Seeing Andrew's face, Mac continued. "You got *called*, dincha, friend? Can't ignore the mountains, y'know. I mean, ya can, but when ya hear the *come and see* you'd be a fool not to go. Guess we all gotta learn that at some point in 'ur lives. As for me, well, I'm no Andrew, but I'm a Macario, which means *blessing. . .* "

Andrew let him talk, saying nothing. He didn't know what to make of this Mac, and he was even less sure he should be following him. But it was night, and he wasn't tired, and he had nowhere else to go. However strange he might be, this Mac character knew his way around, that much was clear. And even if he had an axe strapped to his belt, Andrew felt better about following this stranger than trying to wander through the woods to a different path that might not exist. This path headed straight to the base of the mountain in front of him, and Pearl would be there. She had to be. He would follow Mac until he got there, and then he would go off on his own. Yes. That would be fine.

\*\*\*

It was his daughter who had died, he said matter-of-factly, placing a steaming cup of something that smelled like chamomile in front of him. Andrew took a sip, was surprised to feel the tip of his tongue burn—pain here in this world, even the tiniest pinch, was no less tangible—and sucked hard notes of sweet apple between his cheeks to dispel the sudden heat. They were in Mac's cabin, having walked only another fifteen minutes to the base of the mountains, and Mac had ushered Andrew in without asking if he'd even wanted to enter. A teakettle already sat on a rusting black stovetop, and Mac had grabbed a pack of matches on the wooden mantle, lit the kettle and four lanterns that hung from iron hooks only inches above Andrew's head and along the wall, and swung his pack down before grabbing mugs. He did all this simply by pivoting—everything in the tiny kitchen was practically at arm's length from where Andrew had slumped at the small, rickety table in the center of the room. Soon, the kettle was whistling, Andrew had taken his first scalding sip, and Mac had resumed talking, having only whistled in high, cheery tones during the walk from their meeting spot in the woods.

It was his daughter who had died, Mac said again, as if Andrew had asked. But he said it in the same manner and breath in which he had told Andrew that he had chamomile tea—having not yet taken off his jacket, having not even removed his boots. *It was my daughter who died.* "Foyer information"—necessary information when inviting Andrew in, that information not always commonplace to ask for but expected all the same—like where the bathroom might be. *Across the kitchen, left door.*

And just as that—the bathroom location—wouldn't need elaborating, neither did Mac elaborate on what he had said, instead pouring himself a bubbling mug of water, dropping in a tea bag, and settling into the chair across from Andrew, who remained silent. So small was the kitchen and the table in the middle of it that the two men, leaning forward over their cups, could have knocked heads. Instead, Mac took a sip, smacked his lips, leaned back in his chair, and sighed.

Andrew waited, but Mac only stared at the ceiling, fixating his eyes on the steady lamp burning in the lantern above his head.

Andrew shifted in his seat. Mac had said it so casually, without batting an eye: *It was my daughter who died.* Nonchalant. Still cheery even, a welcome.

*Across the kitchen, left door.*

Mac swirled the tea in his mug and swished what was in his mouth against his cheeks. His eyes were closed now, his head still angled upwards towards the ceiling.

*It was my daughter who died.*

Andrew's thoughts swirled as he stared into his own mug, into the soft orange-brown liquid trapped inside. He closed his eyes, pressing his lids together, willing his thoughts to not go there, not there, anywhere but there.

But there they went. The image of his steaming mug and russet tea faded into the bright fluorescent lights of Pearl's hospital room, to the faded blue knit blanket her sister had brought in a few months before when the chemo had first begun. Pearl was curled up beneath it, her body small under the fabric, her soft hands clutched to her chest, her head angled on the thick, white pillow. The pink-and-blue floral bandana obscured what Andrew knew was beneath—only a few blondish wisps of hair that used to be thick and carefully braided each morning before the garden was pruned.

She was asleep, her lashless eyes standing out against her translucent temples, even while closed. Her mouth was slightly open, as it was when she fell asleep in the middle of the day—something she did more and more towards the end. In these times, because he was always there for them, Andrew liked to pretend she was singing a song. One of her "work songs," the ones she'd hum while pulling up turnips or, if it was autumn, canning apples. In those last weeks, the ones spent in the hospital, he supposed she would be singing "These Boots Are Made for Walkin'," because it was canning season. He kept a fresh jar by her bed—one he had canned all by himself, though he knew Pearl's would have been crisper, cleaner, better. But at least she could smell it, and it might remind her of home.

He hadn't wanted to spend those last weeks that way—trapped in the hospital—and he knew Pearl didn't want to be there, either. *That* was what killed him, really, thinking about what *she* must have thought, thinking about how she'd rather be curled in a blanket in the nylon hammock stretched between the two tallest apple trees, sipping sweet tea out of a long straw, even if it meant she'd die faster. She wanted to die fast—she'd told him herself. If she couldn't live the way she wanted—pulling weeds, crossing streams, climbing mountains—she at least wanted to *die* the way she wanted—at home, however short a time that might turn out to be.

But there was a chance, the doctor had said, and so she was there, in the hospital, a fragile bird trapped beneath heavy blue cloth, always. No outside time, just the slightly open window and, if they were lucky in the sticky heat of July, a soft breeze across their sweating necks. Ultimately, Pearl was a good sport—that was no surprise—and it was often she who was encouraging Andrew, not the other way around. He kicked himself for that now, but it was true:

Sweet, optimistic Pearl, so sure it would get better, so sure that the doctor would let her go home if it wasn't going to, because that's what she wanted, and she'd been sure to tell him.

Andrew had moved past blaming the doctors. They weren't cruel, and they treated Pearl the best they could in those stale, white rooms. He thought they should have known to send her home, but he also knew that they, like Pearl, were optimistic. They, like Pearl, thought it would get better. And so they, like Pearl, were the ones proven wrong.

While the doctors grieved their error, Andrew grieved his wife. He sleepwalked through the funeral, sour notes of "These Boots Are Made for Walkin'" still trapped on his tongue, drowning out hymns like "Blessed Assurance" and "How Great Thou Art." He only barely felt the comfort of the townspeople that had come—almost not registering the men's hands that squeezed his shoulder, the women's cheeks that pressed to his chest when they hugged him. He didn't eat, he didn't sleep, he didn't cry. And when they placed Pearl in the backyard under her hammocking apple tree, he didn't watch. He didn't want to watch his wife move underground to a place she'd never been before. Instead, he'd stared at the mountains across the valley—the ones Pearl had loved to climb—and the river that sparkled between them, bright and shining, defying the darkness of the day.

"Tacito?"

Mac's voice drifted between the mountains still pasted in Andrew's mind and became a breeze that dissolved the snow-dusted peaks. Mac's eyes were no longer on the hissing lanterns above, but instead gazed at Andrew, wide and searching.

"You came to the mountains to find your Pearl, yes?"

Andrew nodded.

Mac swallowed the rest of his tea and peered at the bottom of the cup, as if more would suddenly appear. When it did not, he made a small noise and rose from his chair, turned to the stove, and poured more hot water from the kettle.

"If you were called," said Mac, his back to Andrew, "then ya gotta answer." He collapsed back into his chair, raising a full mug to his lips. Just before taking a sip, he paused, his eyes visible over the rim, locked on Andrew's. "And I'll help ya."

Andrew frowned. Did he really want this man's help? He didn't know Mac at all, and though he was hospitable enough, Andrew hadn't had prolonged company since Pearl had died. Christmases, which they'd usually spent with Pearl's family when they'd come to town, became a drudgery for Andrew, because in the midst of the tinsel and hot cocoa and Pearl's nieces sledding down the hills beyond their little house, Andrew felt only the ache of Pearl's absence. Pearl's family quickly realized his adversity to their visits, and as the years passed, they perfected their excuses to explain why they couldn't make it that year—*Cece might have the flu, Jordan's ballet recital got moved a week earlier, Uncle Jay is moving apartments this week and we have to help*—the excuses weren't very creative, but the delivery was the essential balance between apology and matter-of-factness, and besides, Andrew didn't care to see them—or anyone else—either. They knew it, he knew it, and eventually the whole town knew it, so there wasn't any use in pretending otherwise. Though some townspeople tried at first, as the years passed, nobody visited Andrew, nobody asked why he didn't come in for town festivals or community events the way he used to with Pearl, and nobody made any further attempt otherwise to understand or alleviate his loss.

And now, this timeless lumberjack of a man wanted to help him find Pearl? He had already exhausted his tolerance for other people's company by walking with Mac to his house and drinking tea with him. Andrew wasn't much for talking, but then again, Mac seemed OK with that, or found it endearing, having named him "Tacito." So, if Mac wanted to talk and let Andrew keep quiet as he preferred, was that truly an issue? Besides, Andrew didn't know his way around the mountains—that had been Pearl's forte, not his. In the few times he'd accompanied her on adventures, he'd kept his eyes to the ground most of the time—to keep from tripping—hardly looking around enough to get any helpful sense of the topography of the region. Plus, he wasn't sure how far downriver he'd floated. Certainly far enough that nothing had been recognizable, and he couldn't even see his house. He had the funny feeling, too—though he hadn't acknowledged it until now—that he was somewhere very far from home, whatever that meant. He wasn't a man to dwell on the unknown, and so he pushed the thought from his mind.

Mac's chair scraped against the faded planks of the floor as he stood up. He whistled as he scooped up Andrew's virtually untouched tea and his own empty mug, dumping them in the sink. He turned back to Andrew.

"We'll start in the morning," he said. "It's going to be a long day."

Andrew couldn't help himself. "How exactly will you be helping me?" he asked. "You don't know Pearl."

Mac laughed, deep and hearty. "A man doesn't gotta know another man's Pearl to help him look for 'er," he said, winking and reaching overhead to switch off one of the lanterns. "He's just gotta have the heart to do it." He switched off a second lantern, throwing the kitchen-dining room into half-darkness. The glow of the lanterns along the wall illuminated a small room—from what Andrew could tell, the only other room of the little house—across from the kitchen.

One of them mountains called ya, you say?" Mac's face was cast in shadows, but his eyes shone with a blue light. "Then I s'pose we gotta figure out which one." He paused. Then— "There's a lil bed back there. You can sleep there if ya like," said Mac. "I myself don't mind the floor."

Andrew felt his arms and legs tingle and then sink with heaviness. Pain, fatigue. . . these were still possible in death? If death was eternal rest, as Pearl and her friends from church had claimed it to be, then why was everything still so tangible? Andrew absent-mindedly itched his ankle where the corduroy rubbed. It didn't make sense. . .

"Off ya go," said Mac, switching off the second-to-last lantern.

Andrew rose from the table and shuffled a few steps to the doorway at the back of the kitchen. Sure enough, a twin bed with a thick navy quilt was squished into a small cubby hole, hardly big enough for the bed itself, much less anything else. His joints aching, Andrew sat on the edge of the bed. The mattress was soft and inviting. As he let the rest of his body sink into it, he was reminded of his last sleep, and the gentle cadence of the river as it flowed around him, enveloping his hands and his feet, carrying him along with the current. His hands curled around the quilt, pulling it to his chin like the water that had lapped at his neck as he'd floated downstream the day before. So gentle, so soft it had come, and he had let it. OK.

As his head hit the pillow, Andrew heard Mac's voice ring out from the kitchen, stirring across the surface of the river he felt himself returning to as sleep engulfed him: *One of them mountains called ya, you say? Then I s'pose we better figure out which one.*

# Chapter 5

*The river was safe, and so are the mountains. Do not be afraid. The river carried you here, closer to them, closer to what you seek. You will find it there, in the mountains. Do you believe that?*

*You have to be patient, like the mountains are patient. They have been patient with you, don't you see? Gently they called, earnestly they called, but still they had to be patient, because you would not come, not at first. You doubted them, but they didn't doubt you. And so, they kept calling.*

*These mountains in particular have been here a long, long while. They are used to waiting, to watching their own rocks fall far from them after eons of hanging on. The mountains let them fall, because it is not fruitful to hang onto something that is past its time. But they wait because new rocks form, chiseled by the faithful rain and steadfast wind, forming new ridges and new crevices in their sides, creating landscapes slightly altered from the first landscapes the mountains boasted, even as—at the heart—the mountains remain the same. At their core, they are the same mountains, after all. They know this, and so they let the rocks fall, never complaining, never wanting, never wishing for something different, instead simply standing, steadfast as the rain and wind that beat them to bless them, everything in its time.*

*You are not a mountain, but you have been called by the mountains, and the mountains call only what is their own. Remember that, when you feel discouraged. Remember that, when the rain and winds come, because still they will come, even as you've been called. Remember that—the call of the mountains—when you slip in your search and when you stumble in your ascent.*

*On and on they call, and onward you must go, looking to the ones who've whispered your name, because in them you have your treasure. It is there, waiting for you, if you'll continue to seek.*

*Do you believe that?*

\*\*\*

The light streaming in through the cabin's door reached him where he slept in the bed-sized nook, and his eyes opened. Sleep slipped away like dew melting before the early morning sun, and he was soon able to rise, pleased to notice that his joints did not ache as they had the night before.

Mac was nowhere to be seen. The kitchen, dappled in sunrays, looked equal parts clean and homespun, as if the iron stove's rusting surface had been covered by a thin layer of polyurethane, smooth and clean to the touch but preserving evidence of rust and dirt—good, good use—beneath. On the burner sat the teakettle, still steaming. Mac must have boiled water for morning tea. Andrew helped himself to a cup and was moving to sit at the little table, when suddenly, the front door opened.

"Ready?" Mac's face was beaming, and his dark eyes shone, reflecting the morning energy that streamed into the kitchen in such a way that Andrew wasn't sure if Mac himself had been causing it.

Andrew nodded, not really sure what "ready" even meant, but the dream from the previous night had encouraged him. Today he was one step closer to finding Pearl. That's what the dream had said, at least, and this morning, basking in the steadily warming heat coming from the sun and Mac's eyes, Andrew chose to believe it.

They left Mac's cabin, which, from the outside, had the appearance of a log cabin, except instead of individual logs stacked on top of one another, it seemed to be instead created by the branches and twigs extending from the trees that surrounded it, like it had been swallowed by the woods itself or, more accurately, was just now emerging from them, birthed from somewhere within.

Andrew shook his head and followed Mac, who set off ahead, whistling. The trail had vanished—it was behind them, snaking back into the woods the way they had come the previous night—and now before them lay thinning trees clustered together, growing out of slanted ground, which marked the base of the mountains.

They clambered over thick roots, though they were nothing like the woods through which Andrew had bushwhacked the night before. The morning sun glinted through gaps in the mossy trunks, and Andrew kept his neck ducked towards the ground so as to shield his eyes and let the low-hanging leaves just barely graze his head. He glanced up every now and then, his line of sight moving from the heels of Mac's muddied boots to the back of his black, wide-brimmed hat and red-checkered collar. Each time he did, Andrew had to squint; the sun was gradually rising to a place where its rays couldn't pierce the tree canopies, and yet, somehow, every time Andrew's eyes rose to the back of Mac's head, it was as if the latter's body were a lighthouse—his head the beacon at the top—for the way the sun glinted off of it, bright and unyielding.

An hour passed, and still they walked briskly, ever uphill, creating switchback after switchback, passing two small water runoffs and, at one point, thirty yards to the left, a thundering waterfall—a waterfall so heavy and pounding that Andrew was sure he could feel its spray 100 feet away. Taking only a moment to stare, Andrew plodded faithfully on. His breath came in little huffs, but Mac only continued whistling, his notes clear and loud before they seemed to blend into the sunlight that continually surrounded his head and disappear.

"Where. . ." panted Andrew, ". . . did the path go? Don't. . . other people. . . climb. . . these mountains?"

Mac stopped suddenly, the crescendo of his whistling song halting with him. He turned, a wide smile stretching across his cheeks, and Andrew shielded his eyes. "Sure they do, Tacito," he said. "But only when they've got a reason to. Most people adventure for a while, and then they stop, ya know. Find a place to stay, or move on."

Andrew frowned. "Move on?"

Mac took out a hefty blue water bottle and took several gulps before smacking his lips and replacing the lid on top. "Yessir. Everyone moves on eventually, whether it's here or there. They search a while"—he gestured towards Andrew—"or rest a while, or dream a while, or climb or swim or yell or write or build, and then they figure they better stop that and move on, or keep doin' that and move on."

Andrew frowned. He didn't know what Mac meant by "move

on," since apparently it meant both stopping *and* "keeping on," staying *and* going, which was ridiculous—it had to be one or the other. He said so.

Mac laughed, and the *ha ha ha*'s echoed through the trees. The sunlight danced against the trunks. "Everyone moves on, Tacito. It looks different for different people, but everyone moves on."

Pearl's blue eyes swam into Andrew's mind, and he shook his head, making them dissolve in ripples. He frowned again.

"Did you?" he asked Mac. "Move on?"

Mac had started walking again, and Andrew lurched into a jog to catch up. Apparently Mac had still heard him, because he chuckled in reply.

"Yessir, I think so."

"Then why are you still here?"

Mac made a small noise, something between a laugh and an amused grunt. His arms swung as he walked, picking up the pace, and Andrew, having made the mistake of looking wholly at the back of Mac's head, was blinded and nearly tripped over one of the larger tree roots.

Mac turned his head and yet did not slow down, instead seamlessly stepping over and around a cluster of upright and fallen pines in their direct path. Andrew clambered over the logs, craning his neck to hear what Mac was saying.

"Where do you think we are, Tacito?"

Andrew's mind prickled—the question he had avoided thinking about since circling the invisible fence that surrounded his field back home. He shrugged, then realized Mac had faced forward again. "I don't know," he muttered. "Death, I suppose."

Mac laughed again. "Well, I'll be," he said. "Dead? Really? Well, shoot, death is pretty, isn't it?" He took a deep breath. The pine branches around him seemed to lean closer, their sweet, sharp fragrance making Andrew's nose twitch.

"Well," said Andrew, surprised by Mac's reaction. "Aren't we? Dead?"

Mac stopped again and turned around. He scratched the whiskers on his chin and stared past Andrew, back the way they'd come.

"What makes you say that?" he asked.

What made him say that? Andrew thought back to the invisible fence, to the gently pulling river, to the darkened forest he'd never before traveled through nor seen from a distance.

He thought about before all of that, when, standing in the field, the mountains had first called. *Come*, they'd said. *Come*. And the yellow grasses had rustled, and his corduroy pants had itched. He thought about the man that stood in front of him now, whose bright, grinning face might have been two hundred years old or forty, whose dirt-streaked boots and faded flannel-and-work-pants combination—and, for that matter, his kitchen—looked equal parts lived-in and new. But for all of that, Andrew found himself thinking that he was dead—he had to be—not because of the river or the field or the woods or Mac and his rustic-clean kitchen—but because if he was not, then he would not be here, looking for Pearl. The mountains would not have told him to come, and he would not have, not willingly, unless he was already dead. Only then did he have a chance to find his wife. If he was not dead, then what was he doing here?

Mac nodded at all of this, his eyes the color of the trees around them, glinting with the same light and shadows. He took another drink from his water bottle before offering some to Andrew, who, realizing his thirst, took a sip.

"Tacito," said Mac, his voice quiet. "You believe you are dead because you want to be, and because you are not home in your cabin, surrounded by your fields. You believe you are dead because this is different, because this is unknown."

Andrew said nothing.

Mac moved closer and put a callused hand on Andrew's shoulder. His hand was warmer than Andrew expected, and he flinched. Mac didn't seem to notice, but instead stared at him with mossy eyes that blended into the surrounding trees themselves.

"But Tacito," said Mac, his voice low, his stare unwavering. "I ask you this: Back in your little house, in your yellow fields and turnip gardens and beneath the shade of the apple trees. . . tell me, were you *alive*?"

\*\*\*

Around mid-afternoon, the men made it to the saddle between two adjacent mountains. Andrew wasn't really sure how far or how high they had hiked until there was a break in the treeline. Above them, the trees continued in smaller, shorter clumps, but the dense, twisting roots and the thickest of trunks were now behind them.

Andrew didn't think he would have made it this high this fast if it hadn't been for Mac. Mac moved like the light moved—Andrew couldn't always pinpoint where each step pressed to the dirt; though there were always footprints, Mac's boots seemed to blend into the slanting shadows made by the trees. One moment his foot was pushing off of dirt, and the next moment he was yards ahead, the same leg propelling him from behind a fallen tree trunk. Distracted by Mac's movement, Andrew had lost track of time—he hadn't even noticed his own panting breaths and aching calf muscles.

But the mystery of Mac's travel had worked in Andrew's benefit—though, by stopping, he finally realized his exhaustion, they had made it to the gap between two of the mountains. There, in the break of the woods, Andrew could see the continuation of the peak they were headed towards, grey and jagged at the summit hundreds of yards above them. Across the saddle, another mountain stood, taller than the one they were on, but softer somehow, less abrupt in its ascent. Beyond them, on the other side of the mountain range, more peaks rose—reds and purples and deep grey rock all rising up together, solid and unyielding. These too were dotted black and green with forests, though these were not as dense as the one from which the two men had come. Andrew wondered what was beyond *these* peaks, but their summits were shrouded in swirling white fog, and he could not see beyond them.

His heart sank. The mountain ridge they were on was vast enough; the range of mountains beyond it seemed even more unending. Pearl was in the mountains, waiting for him, and he had no way of knowing which one she might be on. His heart still pounded in his chest, half from tiredness from the recent climb, and half from discouragement—looking at the sheer magnitude and number of the silent, impassive mountains beyond, he couldn't help but wonder if his search was ultimately futile. No. Stop. *Stop.* He'd barely begun looking for his wife. It wouldn't profit to give up before he'd even truly started.

His gaze slid down the side of the mountains they stood between and rested on the expansive valley below. Nestled between this mountain range and the one beyond, about 300 yards beneath the two men, the valley consisted of deep green grass dotted with blue, yellow, and pink alpine flowers. A river, glacial blue and rushing, sparkled from a pinpoint at the base of the far mountains, directly under the soon-to-set sun. The horizon was bathed in golden hour, casting a bronze glow across the currents of the water, which tumbled over itself from the horizon in a rush to break against the treeline below them. Though they were above it now, Andrew realized, the valley had been above *them* for the majority of their day's hike, hidden from sight—still existing, but to them, as nothing. If she had ever climbed this mountain when alive—and he still wasn't convinced this wasn't death—Andrew was sure that Pearl had never mentioned this valley before. How could something so grand, so beautiful, exist without being seen? It was almost unfair.

Watching him, Mac spoke suddenly. "That's the Valley Girl," he said, pointing a long finger towards the trees below the saddle where they stood.

Andrew started. So focused was he on the beauty of the valley that he hadn't even noticed the spectacle directly beneath them, not 100 yards away with the slope of the ridgeline: It was indeed, as Mac had indicated, a girl. She was crouched on a rock—black as obsidian—that was lodged in the middle of the river just before it spilled into the trees. With a jolt, Andrew realized that this must be the same river that coursed near the "path" Mac had trailblazed, and the source of the thirty-foot waterfall he had marveled at hours before.

"She's a good girl," Mac said.

Andrew glanced over. While he had to shield his own eyes against the sun breaking against the horizon, Mac's hands remained at his side. His eyes burned golden, their own small fires. The way he said it wasn't as Andrew remembered people saying it about their dogs—a doting fondness: "She's a good girl"—but rather with a sort of respect, like this small girl crouched on a rock was greater than himself.

"The Valley Girl?" Andrew ventured.

Unexpectedly, Mac snorted. "It ain't like it sounds these days, ya know. Like one of those 'Valley Girls,' with vocabulary fifty percent '*likes*' and thirty percent '*lols*' or '*omgs*' or '*ttyls*'. . . or whatever they say these days." He looked over at Andrew and sighed. "They've butchered her reputation, ya know. She deserves more than that. The Valley Girl's been stopping the Great River from flooding the First Mountains since before anyone here can remember."

Andrew squinted over the ridgeline. He was old, but he was sure the girl below—with her long blond hair and fair skin—couldn't have been more than fifteen. He shook his head. Mac himself could have been any age, and though he didn't know much, Andrew now knew enough about this world he found himself in that he figured it better not to question it. But Mac had said something about the river and the mountains. . .

"The Great River? The First Mountains?" Still holding a hand against the sun, Andrew craned his neck towards the fog swirling across the peaks of the mountains in the distance. "So those. . . are the Second Mountains?"

Mac frowned. "The Third Mountains."

Andrew stared at him. "But where are the Second Mountains?" He hoped against hope that there was not a whole other mountain range to explore.

The sound of Mac's belly laugh echoed throughout the saddle. "Silly Tacito," he said between chortles. "There are no Second Mountains!"

An indignant sound escaped from Andrew's lips. "But—"

But Mac was already waving him off. "The Third Mountains were the original mountain range, here long before even the Great River and the valley and perhaps even the Sun itself. Few folks here know the names and personalities of the characters that inhabit them, or even the identities of the mountains themselves."

"Know. . . the mountains' identities?" Andrew repeated.

"But the First Mountains came second—much, much later," Mac continued, ignoring Andrew's confusion. "After the Great River, and after the valley. They're shaped by the Great River, of course, but it's all thanks to that valley down there." He pointed towards the girl below them, whose head was bowed and almost touching the rock on which she knelt.

"Most valleys are quiet, unassuming," said Mac, staring down at the girl. He looked at Mac, then, and grinned, flashing white teeth. "Sometimes they're a little shy, especially if the mountains around 'em are particularly loud. They take all the spotlight, I guess."

Andrew's head was spinning. But Mac didn't notice.

"The Valley Girl, though, she's special. She bears the brunt of the work, holding back the Great River. Imagine the woods below— and all of us who live there—people and towns and me 'n my hut—if she didn't stay put in that river." He shook his head, still smiling, the fire back in his eyes, a sort of reverence.

Andrew closed his mouth, just then realizing it had fallen open. "Holding back the. . .?" But he trailed off, peering down into the valley, in that moment realizing what he was really seeing: a young girl, yes, blonde and fair, in the middle of icy, swirling currents. But she wasn't crouching on a rock. She *was* the rock. Though he had first thought her legs were bent beneath her, hidden under her torso against a smooth black surface, Andrew saw instead that her torso blended evenly with. . . not a rock, but a thick, black skirt, which was thigh-deep in the glacial river that flowed around her. And it did—flow around her—but the longer Andrew watched, the more he could see the Great River swirling behind her, pushing at her back in waves where she stood firm-footed before it eddied around her and coursed past, but this time more controlled. The Valley Girl was stopping what would surely have been destructive force from crashing over the side of the mountain to flood the world below.

"The river is ice," said Mac quietly, his eyes wide, still staring out across the ridgeline. "It came long before the people here, so it doesn't cater to them. It is ice, smooth and serene. Not heartless, but not compassionate. It didn't know the people, and so it was not born to love them."

Andrew was silent, watching the Valley Girl below. Her blonde hair hung in a curtain around her face, almost touching the river. Right in front of her, directly below her face, the water was still, being the most shielded by the curve of her skirts. There, despite the distance, the water was so clear that Andrew could see that the Valley Girl gazed at her own reflection.

"It seems painful," he said quietly, to nobody in particular. "Like Atlas, holding up the sky to save the world."

Mac grunted. "This ain't like that mythological nonsense," he said, his voice still uncharacteristically low. "But you're right, Tacito. It's hard to be in such proximity to something as cold as the Great River. Valleys are warm, quiet, welcoming. They're self-less, and they love people. They let folks make their homes with them, and they let children play in their green fields, and they let the mountains retain the glory. This here"—he gestured beneath them—"is gentleness submerged in something that existed before community, before warmth. It's foreign, and she takes it, because if she didn't, there'd be no balance. No First Mountains, no woods, no anything else. The Great River would rush on, because it is power, and unseeing. It would surge on because that is what it is, and though it has no motive to, it would destroy us all."

Andrew said nothing.

"Everything must be balanced, Tacito," whispered Mac. "The most powerful things, if contained, can be beautiful. You saw the woods, the waterfall." He gestured back the way they'd come. "But left unchecked. . ." He made a tsk sound and turned back to the valley. Mac raised one hand, which looked darker than usual in the setting sun. Below them, the Valley Girl raised her head. She gave Mac a small smile, the softest of nods, and then Andrew watched as her gaze turned and fell on him. There was so much space between himself on the saddle and the fields and river below, but when the girl looked at him, the whole valley seemed to rise up towards him until he felt that if he were to fall into it, it would catch him. In all of this, the Valley Girl's gaze held him, and looking at her tender smile, punctured by pain and resilience alike, Andrew heard a voice—mild and sweet—ascend to his ears on a breeze infused with the fragrance of alpine blossoms:

*Your grief is powerful, Andrew, and it consumes you. But there is good in it, there can be good in it, in a course directed. Where am I in you, Andrew? Where am I?*

# Chapter 6

*This is your house. Do you recognize it? Yes, you do—the long, single-panel boards, grey-brown after withstanding the sleet of winter and the blaring sun of summer; the faded cotton-blue curtains, which you tied back because they were hers and reminded you too much of her eyes; the cemented foundation of limestone at the base, mottled green and white and rubbed with dirt from the gardens around this little home. You scrubbed this same limestone the summer she died because it was the one thing you could make as good as new. Remember how your fingers bled? Little streaks of red-brown. . . you cleaned that up, too. And the gardens—she would be proud. You made sure that she would be proud.*

*But you hid the curtains, and you got rid of the horses—the ones that she used to ride—because they reminded you of her. The fields are still green, but the grass is long, and it climbs up the fence you put in 365 days after it happened. That fence—the one thing you changed. It keeps people out, right? I'm sorry. . . I'm sorry that you're now one of them.*

*This house, do you recognize it? The gardens are still here, with turnips and tomatoes and carrots and those snow peas she used to eat by the fistful. The apple tree is still there, way out in the field behind the house, and the fraying yellow gingham hammock that ripples in the soft breeze that blows by. The hammock almost scrapes the ground on one side, because ten years ago when that awful August storm crashed through the valley, one of the apple tree's branches snapped and fell, and the hammock caught it, cradling it before it could dash against the cross that marks where she was laid. That was the first time you'd been there since the funeral, wasn't it? Yes. And the last time since.*

*You have the gardens and the house and the tree and the hammock, but you hid the curtains and got rid of the horses. You have the same fields but a new fence. Her hiking boots and trekking poles and gardening gloves, the cribbage set she brought into town every Thursday to play with the girls at church, the mandolin she was given but never learned to play—these things are in the closet in that house. They are contained, though you tell yourself they are treasured. But true treasures are not hidden.*

*You have the gardens and the house and the tree and the hammock, but you hid the treasures and got rid of the memories. Do you recognize this house? Is it the same as before? When the sun shines on it, highlighting the brown-grey of the boards and skimming the grasses that form its skirt, tell me what you see: Everything is neat; there is no clutter. Not even in the closet—that is contained, after all. The grasses blow the same and the tree continually yields apples and you can still smell sweet honeysuckle after morning rain. And oh, the sunsets—those are still faithful, the splash of crimson puckered up against the distant, shadowed mountains; the soft blue of the sleepy sky above, and the pink between that blends it all together. Beautiful. So, so beautiful, and comfortable, too, when you stand in the swaying grass and watch it all.*

*Yes, your house is still there, in the valley and the rolling hills. All comfortable, all just as before. But the horses are gone.*

\*\*\*

The two men had walked the ridge along the saddle and reached the mountain to the left. When Andrew had asked Mac why they weren't going to finish climbing the first mountain—the mountain they'd ascended to reach the saddle—Mac had pointed to the valley, where the small blonde girl stood in the Great River, her skirts billowing around her, the strain on her back—evident only by the white-capped water behind her—balanced by the peace on her face.

"This mountain was just part of the journey," Mac had said. "You climbed the mountain to see the Valley of Rest."

Andrew *had* seen the valley, and the people resting below. The Valley Girl's words came back to him: *Your grief is powerful, and it consumes you. Where am I in you?* He shook his head. He was tired, and her words were puzzling, but he didn't have time for riddles. He had to find Pearl. However attractive rest might seem in the moment—to cradle his head on crossed arms, to incline his face to the sun just like the people in the Valley below—Andrew wasn't ready to give up. Pearl was here. And he had to bring her home—his latest daydream had proven that. His subconscious had conjured up images of his house and his fields and a thousand other things he didn't want to think about, things he missed and things he'd—as the dream had said—put away. He squirmed. Finding Pearl would change that. Things would look different, feel different.

He said this when Mac asked if he wanted to stay for a bit in the Valley. It was a ludicrous question—they'd only just begun, and Mac had promised to help him find *Pearl*, not some Valley Girl. Mac had only nodded in response and set off on the ridge that stretched across the saddle. Andrew tore his eyes away from the valley, away from the blonde head beneath, and focused his eyes on the towering expanse of the summit in front of him. This mountain appeared to be darker than the other one, and it might have likewise been covered in trees, except for the fact that Andrew couldn't see beyond the ridge. The chalky shale of the ridge gave way to patches of dark rock shrouded in fog. Rumbling sounds came from within—was it an avalanche?

"Thunderstorm," answered Mac, but his pace didn't change. He plowed on, the light from his eyes dulling slightly as the first wisps of fog wrapped around his head. Andrew faithfully followed, and the hairs on his arms stood up in response to the dropping temperature. Quickly they were surrounded by the curtain of fog, and Andrew couldn't see five feet in front of his face. He kept close at Mac's heels, panting with the effort as the ground beneath his feet rose in a steady incline—they had left the ridge; they were on the mountain now.

The wind howled and—if it were possible—the fog was thicker the further they climbed. Thunder crashed around them, and the only light that pierced the clouds around them came from intermittent flashes of lightning and, when he turned around, Mac's eyes. Andrew's toes caught on rocks, making him stumble. It was frustrating—all he wanted to do was make it to the summit, to see if Pearl was there, but his mind kept wandering. It was as if every time his feet tripped, his mind was snatched by some other, nagging thought: *Had he locked the house when he left? What about the garden. . . what seeds should he plant next year? Certainly there was more landscaping maintenance to do. . . not to change anything, but to keep it from becom-*

*ing too overgrown and unkempt.* These thoughts were not altogether foreign; in fact, they were reminiscent of a typical day back in his little house—the steady, day-to-day, season-to-season routine that Andrew was sure to maintain. But he didn't want these thoughts now—*now* was the time to focus on finding Pearl, *now* was the time to pay attention to his steps, *now* was the time to follow Mac. . . why were these thoughts intruding? They were comfortable thoughts, and that was what bothered him the most—he wanted to dwell in them, he wanted to be wrapped up by these monotonous, quotidian musings. They were easier, easier than stumbling through fog and searching for his dead wife. Easier than the potential for failure that this adventure offered, easier than hoping. Hope was dangerous. Hope was not certain; these thoughts were certain. He missed certainty. But he also missed Pearl.

Tripping again on an invisible rock, Andrew grunted. In that moment, Mac halted in front of him, and Andrew's face smashed into the first man's back. Mac turned and patted him on the head. "Watch yourself, my friend."

Andrew grit his teeth. "Kind of impossible to do in this fog," he muttered.

Mac looked at him, his eyes beacons against the darkening clouds around them. "Yes, it is, ain't it?" His voice was low, and Andrew heard something else in it, something like sorrow. Or pity.

"Why'd we stop?" Andrew asked.

Mac turned into the fog again, and Andrew's eyes followed Mac's long, checkered sleeve to where his finger pointed, but he couldn't see anything. He squinted. Deep within the fog, a big, dark shape was moving towards them.

"Don't be scared," said Mac, almost shouting so as to be heard above the whipping wind.

Andrew looked down, realized he was clutching Mac's arm, and dropped his hands hurriedly. "Who is it?" he yelled, his voice hoarse.

The big, dark shape kept coming.

"He doesn't see us yet," hollered Mac. "He can't!"

"Who could?" muttered Andrew, but Mac apparently didn't

hear him. A bolt of lightning struck somewhere to their left, followed almost immediately by a cannon-like explosion that shook the ground beneath Andrew's feet.

Whoever this "he" was kept advancing, about thirty feet away from the two men who stood motionless in the storm. The thunder rolled around them, and Andrew was suddenly struck by the fact that, although the thunder and lightning were relentless, there was no rain.

"Tally-ho, friend!" shouted Mac, raising a flanneled arm.

The man, about twenty feet away now, stopped. He raised his head, and an imperceptible sound escaped from Andrew's lips. The man's face was almost translucent, like the fog that surrounded him. Besides Mac (and, if he counted her despite the relative distance, the Valley Girl) this was the first person Andrew had seen up close since he'd left his house in the hills, and, like Mac, the man's clothes appeared both worn and timeless. If this whole world were Death, Andrew decided, then perhaps the people who were here simply wore the clothes they'd died in. But Mac had never said this was Death. Then again, he had never said it wasn't. Andrew peered more closely at the man stepping slowly towards them: He wore corduroy pants and a light jacket. Involuntarily, Andrew's eyes slid down to his own outfit, and his heart skipped a beat. It was nearly identical.

"We are friends from yonder mountain," shouted Mac against the wind, but his indicating arm, Andrew realized, which was stretched towards the mountain they had come from, would have been useless to the man walking towards them because his eyes were halfway closed.

Stopping five feet from them, the man inclined his head towards the newcomers, and Andrew's lips made the same imperceptible sound as before—something between a gasp and a guttural whine. The face of the man in front of him was the most terrifying thing he had ever seen. Indeed, his skin was translucent, and he would have appeared headless in the fog if not for the thick head of jet-black hair, which draped over his shoulders and ran down his back. His half-shut eyes made only his pupils visible—dark wells that sunk into the back of his head. But most unnerving was the man's smile—it was stretched across his white cheeks in a thin line, lips pressed together and upturned at the ends in some sort of sleepy grimace. Andrew had the sense that the man was indeed smiling, but something about the way it appeared made Andrew wonder if his sleep was truly blissful.

The sleeping man's smile broke as he raised his hand. "Hello," he said, and though his voice was musical, the hairs on Andrew's forearms stood up. The man's voice was sleepy too, soft and lyrical— not unlike Mac's, but *unlike* Mac's voice, the cadence of this man's speech was broken at the second syllable: the "o" of *hello* snatched away on the wind in a distinctly minor tone. Andrew was not a hopeful musician like Pearl had been, but it was impossible to miss the haunting melody of this man's *hello*. And yet, the eerie smile.

Mac's response was cheerful, but his face downturned. "Where do you go, my brother?" he asked.

The man cocked his head to the side, and his nostrils twitched as the wind swept up. "Right here," he said, his smile plastered and his eyes unblinking. "Right here is fine."

Mac glanced at Andrew, but Andrew's gaze was fixated on the man's face. And then, again, the corduroy pants. His earlier day-dream swam to the forefront of his mind: The rolling hills of his house, the mossy gate, Pearl's tattered hammock, and the closet . . . the closet, with all of Pearl's things. Andrew blinked.

Mac turned to him, his voice low again, and Andrew had to lean in so as to hear Mac's words before the wind—which was howling now—stole them.

"He is among the most gone of all of them," whispered Mac. "The Forgetting People are all gone to an extent, but this is beyond what I've seen my past travels."

Seeing Andrew's face, Mac continued. "They all smile, the Forgetting People. And you can't call 'em that to their faces, by the way. It would ruin them, because they come here to forget that they're forgetting, and it's not fair for you and I to *remind* them that they're forgetting."

"What are they forgetting?" asked Andrew.

"Whatever they came here to forget," said Mac unhelpfully.

"But—"

"We all got something we wanna forget, Tacito. Another person, a moment, sometimes even ourselves. Wandering helps us forget, because if we wander, our minds wander too, and then we don't have to dwell in what pains us. And so we forget. This man"—Mac gestured towards the sleeping man, who appeared to be (though his eyes were closed) staring at them, but hearing nothing—"This man is hiding from the world and everything in it that makes him remember. Look at him"—Andrew's eyes flicked over Mac's shoulder—"He doesn't look at the other mountains, or the Great River, and he certainly doesn't want to look at the Valley, because the Valley is rest and reflection, even if it has tears, and he can't bear to look at that. It's easier to forget. But forgetting comes at a cost."

"What do you mean?" asked Andrew, wiping his sweating palms against his corduroy pants. A gust blew across his ankles, and they itched again. It took everything in him not to bend down and scratch.

"I mean," said Mac, leaning closer, "that the Forgetting People forget the world and everything in it that hurts them. They forget the icy cold of the Great River that sweeps through the Valley, which would hurt to submerge in but would ultimately refresh them. They don't want the hurt, so they forget it. But neither do they see the Sun. Look at this fog."

Andrew tore his eyes away from the sleeping man and looked around him. He could see nothing. "I don't see anything," he whispered.

"Exactly," said Mac. "Their determination to hide from the world, to forget whatever they want to forget, makes them hidden too. And whatever they wanna forget, or get away from, is only pressed in more against them. And so, day by day, they close their eyes a little more, they walk a little more slowly, their senses are turned off a little more against them. . . all to escape even this enclosure. Their sanctuary becomes their prison."

Suddenly Andrew remembered the first few steps into the fog after stepping off the ridge—how his mind was snatched by thoughts of his house and landscaping and to-do lists, all to keep things as they already were. To maintain the façade that he was OK.

At the last thought, Andrew's throat released a yelp, but it never made it past his lips, which were pressed firmly shut, and slowly upturning at the edges. He grabbed Mac's arm.

"Please, let's leave," he begged, his heart racing, the looming image of the sleeping, smiling man in his periphery even as he still stood there.

Mac gripped his shoulder, his eyes piercing with light against the increasing darkness of the fog. "It's affected you since you stepped foot on this mountain, hasn't it, Tacito? The Forgetting People come to the Forgetting Mountain to forget, but that don't mean they don't think. They only think about what comforts them, whatever distraction they've constructed to help them forget. But they don't know it's a distraction, not until it's too late."

The two men's heads turned in unison to regard the sleeping man before them, whose eyes seemed to shut even more against the wind and fog. Thunder crashed and lightning swirled around them, but the man was oblivious to these things. At half-speed, he raised a massive hand towards his almost pressed-together eyelids, and his smile stretched wider.

"Yes," he said, his voice low and musical as before. "Yes. It is good here. It is a fine place to be."

Andrew's head whipped back to look at Mac. "But, I mean," he said, his voice frantic, "does it matter? He believes he's in paradise, so does it matter if it's really not? He's. . . happy."

The beacons that were Mac's eyes shone, if it were possible, even brighter, and Andrew had to close his own against them. "Tacito," whispered Mac, his familiar musical drawl fading into something that sounded older, years older, aged with pain and loss and the wisdom that came from it. "Tacito, Forgetting People are never truly happy, because they refuse to seek the truth. And they never truly forget, because what pains them also presses upon them, even as they try to forget it. They will only ever forget one thing, and someday very soon: they will forget *themselves* within their own sanctuary, and to forget oneself, Tacito, is worth a thousand deaths."

The wind howled around them once more, and the sleeping man smiled wider. He bent down to the rock shrouded in fog beneath his feet, and he lay down, curled up, and put his head beneath his hands. His eyelids closed the final millimeter between them. The fog surged around him in an instant, wrapping him up. Thunder crashed and lightning struck the blanket of mist that held the man. Andrew closed his eyes against the storm, and when he opened them again, he heard from somewhere within the fog, "*I am fine.*" But the man was gone.

For the first time in twenty-five years since the day his wife had taken her last breath, Andrew sunk to his knees, pressed his hands and his forehead to the fog-swirled ground, and sobbed.

***

As the two men descended the south side of the mountain, the fog faded, and the setting sun sank low towards the valley where thousands of people knelt, rested, laughed, and cried. The golden orange of the sunset flashed across the stormy waves of the Great River and tangled in the brilliant yellow of the Valley Girl's hair, which still pooled across the current, rippling with power.

Mac led Andrew down the Forgetting Mountain's back side as a father guides a small child through a crowd. One of Mac's hands on his elbow, the other at his back, Andrew let himself be held as he stumbled over boulders and coughed on kicked-up dust. His eyes watered, partly from the terrain and partly from the memory of the Forgetting People, and the vanished man, whose forgetfulness had seduced him and consumed him, reducing him to less than he was . . . until he, quite simply, was not.

In Andrew's mind, the little cabin on the hill—his home and refuge—loomed. The picture he had always maintained—the one of goldenrod-scented sunsets and light breezes and cozy fires within—was tainted. It was as if someone had taken a match to the edge of the portrait in his mind, letting the borders blacken and curl, slowly eating away at the memory it held. The house itself was dark, windows shut, curtains hidden, jars of preserves in the cellar unopened and dusty. No fire burned in the hearth, and the air was stale and stagnant. Only the closet was open and gutted, items spilling from its inside: boots, poles, gloves, a cribbage set, a mandolin, books, stacks of church bulletins, a secondhand leather purse from Italy.

Seeing Pearl's old things—even in his mind—made Andrew's gut wrench and his heart throb. More tears welled beneath his eyelids, and he blinked them back, but the picture would not go away. Even so, despite the rawness of the closet and its contents, despite the harsh, blinding light that poured from the closet that spilled them, Andrew didn't want to look away. The rest of the house and the field and the hills were blackened and bare, and though they were the *same*—all comfortable and familiar—they held nothing for him. What was once soothing to him was now colorless, a dark grey, tinged with the slightest green. Cold, quiet. Eerie. The vacant, expressionless comfort scared him now. There was no memory of Pearl in these things.

And Andrew realized: For twenty-five years, he had hidden Pearl's things away, shoving them in closets and cupboards—away, away—all to forget the memory of her death, ensconcing himself in the house they shared together, the garden they built together, never dwelling in these things and their relation to her, but simply existing within them. But in doing so, Andrew had not only immersed himself in the act of forgetting Pearl's death; he had, in fact, succeeded in forgetting her *life*. All this time, he had been trying to cling to her, to preserve her, but he had only shut her away from himself and the rest of the world. She was dead, and he had killed her memory, too.

"Where are you, sweetheart?" gasped Andrew, choking back another sob. "Where are you, my Pearl?"

Catching his toe on a rock, Andrew lurched forward, but Mac steadied him without missing a step. Clutching Mac tighter, Andrew plodded on, down, down, down and away from the Forgetting Mountain.

"I'm sorry," he whispered into the wind, but, eyes burning and mind swirling once more with the smoldering image of his once-beloved home, he wasn't quite sure whom he was talking to.

# Chapter 7

It was time for another mountain, Mac said, because it was clear that Andrew wasn't going to find Pearl among the Forgetting People. So, the two men bent their knees and half-walked, half-jogged to the base of the treeline on the south side of the mountain they had just climbed. Down below the ridge, the fog was nowhere in sight. Birds chirped, and Andrew could hear the soft sound of water trickling over fallen branches somewhere to their left. Above them, he knew, over the ridge, the Great River coursed, cool and unthinking, and still the Valley Girl would be, too, parting and slowing the mighty waters to save the people searching or meandering below—people like him.

They seemed to be in the same forest they had been in a few days ago, the one they'd traveled through when first leaving Mac's timeless hut. But they'd come down the back of the Forgetting Mountain, not the way they'd come. This, then, had to be a different set of woods, with the Valley somewhere to their right. From the ridgeline the day before, looking out over the Valley, Andrew had seen a second set of mountains. Or, rather, a. . . "Third" set.

"Are we headed to the Third Mountains?" Andrew asked Mac, the latter of whom was several paces in front of the first, and not nearly as out of breath.

Mac chuckled. "I ain't never been there myself," he said, his voice neglecting the older, wiser tone he'd assumed earlier, when Andrew had asked about the Forgetting People. Back in the woods, Mac was clearly at home, and Andrew could have easily been with a friend in the forest south of his own valley back home—the woods that separated his cabin from the town he and Pearl used to regularly visit. But, of course, he hadn't really had a friend in twenty-five years. Pearl had been his only, really, though he'd often visited with the husbands of her girlfriends if they had been attending a housewarming or holiday party, or if they ran into each other while running errands. Even then, Andrew hadn't spoken much, though he'd been happy to listen to fishing or hiking stories or whatever the other men were discussing while Pearl happily caught up with her own friends. One man in particular—the husband of Suzanne, Pearl's closest friend—was one for whom Andrew, over the last decade of Pearl's life, had developed some fondness. This man was quieter than the others, less boisterous and not as proud, who often adopted a listening role if other men were present, except of course, when the only other man was Andrew. If Suzanne and Pearl were chattering away in the middle of the pharmacy, Andrew and—what *was* his name?—would stand in comfortable silence together until the other man made a light remark about his maple syrup business back home, the odds and ends that that entailed, and whether or not Andrew might ever want to see it. Andrew never did see it, and Suzanne's husband didn't push, but the topic became a comfortable place to start whenever their wives ran into each other at the store or after church.

What *was* the man's name? Andrew frowned. And it dawned on him—Ernest. Yes, Suzanne and Ernest Endelway. As he plodded through the lush, green underbrush, Andrew found himself wondering what Ernest Endelway was up to these days, and whether or not he was still making syrup. Andrew had meant to try it, and to visit their farm, but Pearl and Suzanne often preferred to embark on adventurous escapades in the mountains or run errands together rather than visit one another's homes. When Pearl had died, Suzanne had come around a few times with homemade meals, her own eyes welling up and the rest of her face consumed with grief, but after a while, she'd stopped. It was Andrew's fault, really—he had never invited her in, and when she'd tried to ask him how he was, he'd simply grunted and looked down, waiting for her to stumble through a tearful goodbye and step down from his porch. If Suzanne saw him running errands, she'd always approach and give him a hug, but Andrew never said a word beyond the mechanical, obligatory "hello." Eventually, Suzanne and all the others who Pearl had known—either only by face or quite well—stopped asking and stopped dropping by. Little by little, Andrew stopped going into town. He grew what he could, saved almost everything, and had his necessities shipped. He didn't see any of Pearl's friends beyond the first year after her death, and he never saw Ernest Endelway.

Andrew shook his head. He didn't know why he was thinking about Ernest Endelway over twenty-five years later. The man could have died, or moved, or was now in the hospital, and there was really no way to know.

"You haven't been to the Third Mountains?" Andrew called out, trying to force the image of Ernest and Suzanne from his mind.

Mac obliged. "I sure haven't. Nobody has. Nobody who's still here, anyway." Looking at Andrew's concerned grimace, Mac chuckled and continued, "Nah, Tacito. I don't mean like that—that people wander off to the Third Mountains and disappear. If you're goin' there, you *mean* to go there, you know what I mean?"

Andrew did not.

"Let me put it this way, Tacito. You get to the Third Mountains when you're done with the First. When you've climbed and sojourned and lived here long enough, or when you've rested with the Valley Girl long enough to process whatever brought ya here in the first place. . . well, it's then that you just kinda move on."

Mac sat down on the woods floor, leaning on a large, mossy boulder that was half-concealed in a thicket of pines. Andrew slumped down next to him, his muscles throbbing from the morning's long descent. His legs and arms told him he wanted to sleep, but he knew he could not; his mind was racing.

He looked at Mac. "And you. . . you haven't?" His own question surprised him; he realized he had never asked Mac why he was here, in the First Mountains, and seemed to have been here for quite some time. The other man's face was hidden in the shadows of the pine branches, but sunlight streamed through the needles, throwing a razor-thin stream of white across Mac's eyes. His pupils were dark but warm, seemingly absorbing the light and yet throwing it back at Andrew in kaleidoscopic color. Reds and oranges refracted from Mac's unblinking stare, piercing the shadows formed by the trees around him and forcing Andrew to blink. But, even when he closed his eyes, Andrew could see the rainbow in his vision, and Mac's green eyes, growing lighter by the second, continued to strike him through the colors.

A smile, equal parts wistful and hopeful, broke across Mac's face, and his voice rang out through the kaleidoscope of color, finding Andrew's ears and blocking out all else—the birds, the flow of the streams, the wind—like Andrew was wearing a giant pair of headphones. Even with his eyes closed, Andrew still saw Mac, and heard his voice, golden like the sun, and perhaps just as old, each word followed by the faintest echo.

*Her name is Julia. When I lost her, she was eight years old.*

(Behind Andrew's closed eyes, the forest surrounding Mac flattened, and up sprung a small town: a bright red general store, a small schoolhouse, a church, and several small cottages clustered in the town square. A small, tan-skinned, dark-headed girl with pigtails and a bright purple skirt jumped rope alone in the dust of the school playground. Her black shoes were scuffed with dirt, but she was smiling, and singing loudly—a song Andrew had heard a long time ago near the schoolyard of the town he and Pearl had once been a part of.)

*Julia. Sweet Julia. She was so loud, that girl, and so full of life. She played with everyone in her class, always including the others, but even when she was by herself, she had no less fun. I loved to walk to school after work—I worked long hours at the lumberyard, so she had to wait for me—but every time I came, she would be throwin' that rope and singin' a song.*

"Papá!" the little girl shouted, dropping the fraying rope into the dirt and running towards Andrew. Andrew saw his arms, wearing the same red-and-black checkered sleeves Mac still wore, reach out towards the little girl and hug her warmly when she collided with his chest. She smelled like green apple shampoo, and faintly of Play-Doh. Andrew thought he would recoil at the physical touch, but something welled inside of him—a warm, heartbreaking fondness. He wasn't a father, but it was unmistakable, this feeling—the feeling of hugging his own daughter—the only daughter he had.

Through the vision, Mac's green eyes flashed something—a soft pain, dulled by time but still present.

"Mija!" Andrew felt his mouth say, his voice warm and jingling—unmistakably Mac's.

*We always did puzzles at home after school, or made tamales, her favorite snack.* (The vision changed accordingly, showing Julia in a little pink apron with a scruffy-looking unicorn on the front pocket. She stood at a wooden counter in a small kitchen not unlike the one Andrew had seen in Mac's house that first night before their mountain journey. She held a spoon with corn *masa* caked on the end, and she was looking up at Andrew, brown eyes shining. Andrew's arm reached over and wiped some *masa* off of her nose. She giggled.)

*But Julia's favorite thing was to visit her* abuelo. *My father. He lived a few towns over, by himself in a little cabin. He fished and sold the fish to the local grocery store every Monday, and that was enough for the week. I grew up in that house, and I loved it, too. But Julia and I, after she was born, had to move out, at the time for Julia's mother's sake. My father understood, on the condition that we visit him every Monday after his trip to the store. He always kept some of the week's catch and fried it up for us.*

*It was Monday, after school, after tamales, after the fish sales. Julia had saved a few of her own bean tamales to bring to Abuelo's, and we got in the car.*

Andrew's hands held the steering wheel of a rusty, red Ford two-door. Julia sat next to him on the brown cloth seats, wearing too-big sunglasses and singing along to the radio. A Spanish singer hummed a tune Andrew did not know, but Julia's sweet soprano made the corners of his mouth turn upwards. Sun streamed through the dusty windshield, and the road in front of them curved with the river.

*It was a beautiful drive to Abuelo's house—one I'd driven a thousand times before. Every week. The same winding road, the same sparkling river where his weekly catch came from, the same swaying grasses. Everything about this road was familiar. The late evening sun was the same, and it was tricky to drive in with the trees casting their shadows across the road—right where it bended—makin' blind spots even with my big windshield. But I had done it a thousand times before.*

Andrew's hands turned the steering wheel to the right, following the curve of the white lines on the blacktop. The sky was a deep blue, and Andrew had lived in this region long enough to know that it would fade quickly to dark once the sun touched the horizon. He figured it would be about an hour. Shadows danced on the yellow lines. He blinked and drifted over the centerline. He corrected, understanding what Mac meant. This light was tricky. But the truck felt familiar, and Julia was singing, and they were going to *Abuelo's*. It was going to be a good evening.

*It was going to be a good evening. Julia loved her abuelo. He loved her. His face lit up every time we stopped by.*

Fuzzy at first in Andrew's mind, a face swam into clarity: A big white mustache covering thin lips, eyes green like Mac's (but much older) and crinkling at the edges. The mustache quivered—the man was smiling. Julia's laughter rang in the background—*Abuelo!*—and the man's smile widened. The same warm feeling from before spread through Andrew's chest. The vision shimmered, and he was back in the truck, with Julia in the passenger seat, driving the two of them along the same country road.

*This day was no different. Same road, same light, same shadows. I don't even know what happened. But something happened. It was too quick for me to understand, and too abrupt for me to fix.*

The mood in the truck shifted suddenly. The clouds seem to darken, the lines on the road grew brighter, and the shadows lengthened. Julia's singing was the same—bells jingling in Andrew's ears—but it became an echo as his vision darkened. . .

The truck drifted sideways, crossing the centerline again as the road took a sharp bend to the left. Headlights shone into the windshield, dousing the brown interior in a deep gold, like sunbath. It was warm and swirled with the shadows—beautiful, really—but why were there headlights? That could only mean. . .

Julia's singing broke then, and her sweet voice lurched upwards into a high-pitched scream. Andrew's right arm flung sideways, his checkered sleeve catching Julia's chest and pinning her to the back of the passenger seat, his other arm yanking the steering wheel sideways in a last-ditch effort to avoid the oncoming car. . . A horn blared out of the shadows, but he didn't know if it was his or the other's. . . tires squealed. . . tree branches bent down to meet them. . .

*And it was dark. Everything was dark.*

Andrew's eyes opened, and he was leaning against the boulder in the woods, hands clenching the dirt. He spread his fingers into the ground and looked up at Mac. The rainbow of color was gone from Mac's eyes—they were once again a piercing green. The same flannel from the vision—the one Andrew had worn—was sitting in front of him now, worn by the other man, whose arms were crossed over his chest.

Mac sighed. "I couldn't do nothing, Tacito. Not a damn thing."

"And that's how. . .?" Andrew's voice faltered, and wiping his hands on his corduroy pants, he realized he was sweating.

"Yes, that's how she died."

Andrew swallowed. He wanted to ask how the *abuelo* had reacted, if Mac had called an ambulance, how the news had been delivered, how Mac had felt. . . all of those things. But he didn't, because all he could think about was the doctor from that one night in July a couple decades before, his straight face but pitying eyes, and the flatness with which he delivered the news, because there was really no other way to deliver it but business-like—a transaction that transmitted the message's finality, because if it didn't, it would create questions and possibly a little hope, and make the news just that much harder to process.

"I'm sorry," murmured Andrew, because that was really all he could say.

Mac nodded, his eyes down. "Me too, Tacito, me too. For a while I was here searchin' for her, for my Julia, just like you're searchin' for your Pearl. But eventually, I stopped searching." He looked at Andrew and continued, "Oh, not because I gave up. Ultimately, I spent a stint in the Valley and I realized somethin'—I'll see Julia again. She just ain't here."

Andrew squirmed. Mac seemed OK with that fact, but it bothered him. What if that were true about Pearl—that she wasn't here? He hadn't really let himself consider it before, but now, with Mac sitting in front of him, he had to wonder if that were true. What if he was searching for nothing?

Mac seemed to read his thoughts. "Now, that's somethin' I realized for myself. Julia is in the Third Mountains—that's where they all go eventually, the ones who have left us to go to a better home. But that don't mean Pearl is one of them, at least not yet. She could be here—or she could not be—but that's somethin' only you can figure out."

Andrew took a deep breath. "But if you know that's where your daughter is. . . then why aren't you there, too?"

Mac looked at him again, his eyes growing brighter. Andrew looked away, but he could still feel Mac's stare on his temples, like the handprint of the sun on a hot day. "Because I have to be here," he said, his voice soft then, and older. "I am here to be Macario. . . a blessing. And until the Third Mountains call me home, here I'll be."

Mac stood up, apparently ready to go again, but Andrew's head was spinning. The First Mountains had called him. He was meant to be here. He thought it was to find Pearl, but what Mac had said made him stop. What if Pearl were not here, and he was here for some other reason? His heart hurt in his chest. He had no other reason. He knew no other reason. He only knew Pearl, the life they had once had, and how much he yearned for that again. He didn't care where—life or Death, or whatever this world was—he only wanted to be with her.

"Let's go, Tacito," Mac whispered, his face lost in the light and shadows somewhere above where Andrew still sat. "We must keep looking."

Andrew shakily got to his feet. "Yes," he murmured. "We must keep looking."

***

The Sun had fallen, and the two men were far enough away from the Valley that they could no longer hear the rumble of the Great River, nor see the soft green grasses or glimpse the people sprawled in them, faces to the sky. The night was cold, but the stars were out, brighter than Andrew remembered them. How many nights had he been here? It had seemed so long since he'd left Mac's cabin. . . when had that been? A few days ago, or a week? But this was the first time on the journey that he remembered the sky growing dark. Could it really have only been a single day?

In front of him, Mac moved silently, his feet gliding over the tree roots. Without the Sun in the sky, Mac looked even brighter—a fine, white glow surrounded his body and pulsed as he walked. Andrew kept his eyes fixed on Mac's red-and-black flannel, a sight that had grown so familiar to him, and comfortable somehow, like his cabin—whose corners still burned in his mind—had once been. But unlike his secluded property, Mac was here, and alive. Something like a friend, someone to talk to. Andrew's heart seemed to beat louder, and he swallowed. It had been so long.

"Ho, there!" shouted Mac suddenly, and Andrew was snatched out of his thoughts. Instinctively, he lurched back—when they'd come across the last person on their journey, he'd eventually disintegrated into the fog. Andrew wasn't sure what to expect on this new mountain, even at its base.

But it appeared that Mac hadn't been shouting at anyone. He turned around to face Andrew. "Look!" he said, his eyes gleaming, and pointed.

Through the trees a short distance away, in the middle of what seemed to be a large glade, a bonfire burned. Shadows moved in front of it—people? There were many of them, all clustered near the fire, passing around what seemed to be—Andrew squinted—plates of food. Shouts of laughter arose from the smoke, which curled high above the pines and was absorbed by the stars.

"What is. . ." Andrew's voice was soft—he didn't want to disturb them, but he also didn't want to inhibit their joy from reaching his own ears. It was refreshing, to hear their tinkling voices, broken by sudden peals of laughter, and the clatter of sticks on stones as they stoked the fire.

Mac's eyes still shone. He answered Andrew, but he kept his gaze on the scene. "The Wildering People."

Andrew recoiled. "'Wildering' people? Like they 'confuse' you? Lead you astray?"

Mac chuckled, and the trees seemed to bend down, laughing

with him. "No, Tacito. The Wildering People are only named as such because, by their ways here, they bewilder those who are still journeying. These people live here, in this little village, together. They've made a community, and that usually doesn't happen here."

"Why not?" asked Andrew, his eyes on a small group of children that danced by the fire.

"Because," said Mac. "Most people here in the First Mountains are looking for something, or someone. They are either looking, or they're resting in the Valley. Very infrequently are people *living* here intentionally for no other purpose than to live."

Andrew had so many questions that he didn't know where to start. "Live" here? In Death? Why would these people choose that? Why didn't Mac?

Right on cue, Mac looked at him. "For a time I considered it, Tacito. The Wildering People are the kindest, most welcoming people I've encountered here in the First Mountains, and they invited me to stay. I almost did, but then. . ." he trailed off.

"What?" Andrew prompted.

Mac just looked at him. "You," he said simply.

"Me?" It came out incredulous.

"Yes," said Mac. "I was told you would be here."

"Who? Who told you?"

But Mac had apparently exhausted the subject—his gaze was back on the Wildering People, and his voice was once again a familiar, somehow jingling drawl. "Well, I reckon. . . it couldn't hurt. . ."

And, without warning, he had set off again, and Andrew's legs involuntarily stumbled after him. Mac drifted through the remaining trees separating them from the glade, and then, quite suddenly, they were there.

There was music, and dancing, and—Andrew had been right—lots of food. Some type of meat, seared over the fire, floated past his nose on tin plates. Cups of a boiling, cinnamon-scented drink swirled around him, hands taking and passing and taking and passing again. Children tossed a knitted ball—something like a hacky-sack—between them in a large group, shouting something incomprehensible every time another caught the ball between his knees instead of his hands. When that happened, the other children fell on the ground instantly, rolled over a few times, and bounded back up in time to catch the hackysack before it hit the ground.

Older members of the community reclined in wooden chairs by the fire, speaking in vibrant voices. Andrew peered closer—there was no wood fueling the fire, but simply dark, obsidian rock at its base. When the people sitting near the fire laughed, the flames leapt higher, crackling and spitting—almost chuckling—against the midnight-blue sky.

"Friends!" said Mac to the nearest cluster of elders.

They stopped mid-conversation and turned, smiling widely. "Macario!" said one with long grey hair and a russet-brown shawl. "We were hoping you'd be back soon! And who have you brought with you?"

"This," said Mac, gesturing behind him to where Andrew hovered, heart beating fast, "is Tacito." Andrew couldn't help but notice how Mac's voice shone with pride, and he felt a wave of fondness wash over him.

"Tacito," said the elder, looking at him. When the man's gaze met his own, Andrew's skin tingled. It felt as if a thousand eyes were lightly dancing over his whole body—really, truly seeing him. In his mind, he saw himself at three years old, hovering on the edge of an old bridge in his backyard, and his mother—long skirts swooshing—running across to grab him before giving him a good spanking. The vision flashed, and he was fifteen, leaning against the schoolyard fence, watching the girls in their pressed white uniforms pass by, and he and the other boys with him hollered. The image flashed again, and things moved more quickly now: He was twenty-five, staring into Pearl's blue eyes beneath her wedding veil, feeling his lips form the words "I do"; he was fifty and they were horseback riding, the two of them laughing at the way the horses whinnied back and forth in their own conversation; he was fifty-five, and Pearl was sick, laying in the hospital bed with whiter-than-snow skin. . .

Andrew blinked, his own skin feeling warm and raw. The elder was still smiling at him, and his eyes were kind. "Welcome, Tacito," he said. "We are the Storytellers, and we welcome you."

# Chapter 8

This house was large—three stories, with vaulted ceilings and floor-to-ceiling windows in the great room, where a stone fireplace towered—a sturdy backbone, holding everything together. The walls, the color of slow-churned buttercream, were almost obscured by portraits—painted and photographed—of several different people: old, black-and-white portraits, with children playing together on a seesaw, their knee-high socks crisp and clean; old-time photographs with a stern-looking woman with a tight, high bun in her hair, hands primly folded across her lap in front of her softer, rounder husband; newer paintings of rosy-cheeked girls in blond pigtails, holding bright red lollipops and smiling up at the artist. The people in these portraits were all different—young men with suspenders, old women with sweeping skirts, children with high-waisted shorts and soccer cleats—but each face, if you looked closely, was characterized by the same small, button nose whose nostrils turned up slightly higher than most.

This house belonged to the Boulder family, passed down for generations. Over time, its walls stayed the same creamy white, but each generation, each year, new photos and paintings were added, or the cupboards were updated, or the couch was upholstered to hide the weathered red velvet that Samson Boulder, Sr., had refused to change during the entirety of his sixty-seven years on Earth. These changes brought a flare of revolution, and just a little bit of awe, but not so much that the house's foundation was betrayed. Honor, diligence, and—most of all—family loyalty characterized the grand staircase that swept up from the foyer, and moved through the robust copper piping from basement to the third floor where the children's rooms were, all the way out to the stables where at least two horses lived at all times, from the moment Samson Boulder, Sr., built the house until the fire demolished the whole thing after the birth of the seventh generation.

Before the fire, the house had only one scare of falling from the Boulder family's possession: When the youngest son, Edmund Jr., fell in love with Miss Delilah Beaucourt, daughter of his father's steel business competitor, the house thought for a moment that it would become collateral as part of Mr. Beaucourt's reluctant agreement to marry his daughter to an ostensibly lower (than his) class man. It would have been the opposite of a dowry—the exchange of the Boulder house for the Beaucourt daughter—but Edmund Sr. would have done it for his son, because it would have fulfilled the first Boulder family pillar: family loyalty. Luckily, however, Miss Delilah ran away with Edmund before her father could have demanded anything of the sort, and the house remained intact and Boulder-held. Everyone knew the Beaucourt daughter had run to the Boulder house to marry Edmund Jr., but Mr. Beaucourt kept it as quiet as he could—which is to say, out of the newspapers—by not making a fuss about the Boulder house deed, as everyone thought he might. It was all very strategic, and because the Boulder house remained a stalwart, uncontested symbol of the town, everyone agreed to forget about Miss Delilah's betrayal. Soon, she was a Boulder, her portrait was added to the house's walls, and she, too, became something of a legend.

Indeed, the house remained strong and intact over the generations before the fire, even if it did succumb to the general wear-and-tear that every house experiences, especially when Miss Delilah had her triplet sons—Edmund III, Curtis, and Casper. The three boys had elfish ears and the same famous Boulder nose, and their eyes twinkled in unison. They were boisterous boys, but the town loved them because their antics were, in the long run, harmless. But when they created a jungle gym out of the house's 17th-century French chandeliers on the second story, Miss Delilah had no choice but to ship them off to military school until they came back with sturdy jackets and pressed pants, albeit with the same devilish twinkle in their eyes.

Still, no one expected the fire, right at the turn of the sixth-to-seventh generation. Edmund III's wife, a young French girl he had met while stationed abroad after military school, died while giving birth to their only son, Samson, and Edmund III refused to remarry. Some said it was the lack of female presence that started the fire—the house was unbalanced—while others said it was the inauspicious naming of the child to be the same as that of the original builder of the house, since it created a full circle, a sort of end to a beginning. But whether it was Edmund III's stubbornness that killed the house, or the fateful naming of his son, the house burned before young Samson could marry and swing in the eighth generation.

The cream-colored walls, still vibrant despite their age, curled in the smoke, the copper piping melted, the stables went up in flames, and the only thing left standing from the multi-generational house was the stone fireplace. As the smoke subsided, the Boulder boys were coming home from an afternoon horseback ride. Lucky—Sam's pony—and Charlie—Edmund III's mare—stood still in the ashes, their ears flickering nervously. Sam wanted to cry as the final boards fell, but he could only stare, stunned, at his father's expressionless face. The wind was quiet, and the crackling of the embers around the burned chandeliers was the only thing to be heard in the otherwise deafening silence. Sam figured his father would fall to his knees, or command Sam to do something with the horses before whipping into action himself, but all Edmund III did as he and his only son stood in the ashes was make a small noise in his throat before opening his mouth. "Well, that's that." Sam was too young to hear all the stories the house had held for the Boulder family over the last few hundred years, but he was not so young that he could not sense the gravity of the situation and realize his own marooned state—the only Boulder male in seven generations to not assume the sacred family sanctuary.

For his own part, Edmund III kept it together, but the twinkle in his eye was less pronounced for the remainder of his life, which was only five more years after the literal familial pillars fell. Young Sam was thirteen years old when his father died. He lived with his father's friend until he was eighteen, finished school, and himself went to the military. The officers recognized the Boulder family twinkle, but there was no house to speak of, no family loyalty to speak of, because Sam was all that was left. He did what he could to keep the other pillars close to his heart—always putting honor and diligence first, first in the military and then as a self-started carpenter. He married for love, which felt loyal to his grandpa's own marriage, and that was that. Gone was the Boulder house—the symbol of the Boulder legacy. But, again, Sam kept the house close to his heart, and passed its pillars on to his children. And he died, after eighty-seven years, in the small cabin he and his wife had built together decades before, only a miniscule remembrance of the magnificent house that had raised the Boulder family for 300 years.

\*\*\*

The fire was small as the elder finished his story. He wrapped his russet-brown shawl tighter around him and raised his gaze to

Andrew, who sat cross-legged next to Mac by the flickering coals, which did not burn him.

Andrew's mind shimmered with the image of the house from the story—tall, cream walls and thousands of portraits of loved ones and moments aligned with precision against them. He thought of the way the house had fallen, several generations of use crumbling within hours. A tear fell from his eye, and he wiped it away hurriedly. It wasn't so much the story as the way the elder had told it, his voice low and musical, captivating, blocking out every other thought Andrew might have had before. So this was why the Wildering People were the Storytellers. As Andrew stared into the crackling fire, he saw dancing images: three triplets swinging from chandeliers; a young woman fleeing from her own mansion, crossing the stream to a multi-generational home; a hammer swinging down on a nail to raise the first wall of that same house.

"Thank you, Sam," whispered Mac, his own eyes shining as he looked at the Storyteller with the long, grey beard.

"*You're* Sam? Sam from the story?" asked Andrew, his mouth gaping.

The russet-shawled elder bowed his head in assent.

"But. . . I don't understand," said Andrew, almost to himself. "Didn't that. . . did that. . . scar you?"

The elder—Sam—smiled. "A freak fire burning down a generational home before I could have it for my own, continuing long-standing tradition? Of course, in some ways." He chuckled, and the fire spurted upwards. "But Tacito," he continued, and his voice seemed to wrap Andrew in warmth greater than that of the flames he sat by. "What did the story do for you?"

"For me?" Andrew's brain whirled, scrambling to come up with something. An elder near him—a man with short, salt-and-pepper hair and a green shawl—touched his shoulder, and the whirling in Andrew's mind stopped. He felt calm.

"I suppose," he said, and coughed, aware that all eyes were on him. The children still played in the background, but their voices were muted. "I suppose. . ."

Andrew thought back to the story, and emotions surged in his heart again—sorrow for the loss of the house, and then a static, dull pain, followed by a deep nostalgia. Then, after those, his heart felt still again, a peace punctured only sporadically by softened throbs, and yet even these seemed eons apart.

"I feel like I understand," he whispered then, and his heart thudded, because he realized the truth of his words. He *did* understand. He understood all of it, except the last part—the peace. That felt strange—wonderful, but strange. Foreign, after so many years.

"I believe you," said Sam, looking straight into Andrew's eyes. There was no pity in them, not like Suzanne's that first year after Pearl's death, not like the sweeping gazes of the townspeople before Andrew stopped going into the community and instead retired completely from the public eye. Instead, Sam's stare was only that of empathy. The loss of his house surged with other losses—the loss of his family legacy, the loss of his father, and, to some extent, the loss of himself. Andrew's mind flashed back to the Forgetting Man—the one who had vanished into the whipping storm only the day before—and Mac's words: *To forget oneself, Tacito, is worth a thousand deaths.*

Andrew looked around him. The other four elders that sat in the circle were all looking at him with the same soft smile. But again, it wasn't pity. Andrew's eyes drifted upwards, and above their heads, framed against the firelight, were soft orbs, shimmering as the smoke moved behind them. In each orb was a scene: In one elder's, a young baby sleeping in a crib; in another's, a professor's desk laden with papers and books; in another elder's orb—one who, Andrew noticed then, was in a wheelchair—there only seemed to be himself, with two perfectly functioning legs; in Sam's orb, the Boulder home. Andrew looked next to him. Mac had an orb too, and inside was an image Andrew had seen earlier—two hands gripping its steering wheel as young Julia bounced in the passenger seat, pigtails swinging and voice singing. Above him, Andrew's own orb sparkled: There, relaxing in her hammock, trekking poles resting against the tree, sat Pearl, blue eyes shining as she wiped her forehead and sighed, the day's long adventure reflecting in the sweat that beaded her brow. Andrew's lip quivered, and he grit his teeth.

But, looking around at the Wildering People, and at Mac, Andrew had never felt so understood, or so unashamed for the image that coursed through his mind and in the orb above his head. These men knew what he had gone through, for they had all lost something, too: a loved one, their ability to move, their career. But the orbs that held these images were not dull, nor filled with sorrow, as Andrew expected them to be. Tinged, maybe, but not filled. Over everything else, the images in the orbs were vibrant—full of life.

"Words resurrect the dead," said Sam, the house above his head shimmering still. "And stories give them a place to stay."

The fire crackled, and Andrew looked up once more at the image in his own orb. Pearl was smiling, her face tilted up to the sun that streamed through the tree branches above her hammock. Andrew's heart tugged—a sharp pain at first, but before he could push the image away, Sam's hand was on his shoulder.

"Wait," he said, eyes serene. "Just wait. Look past the pain."

Andrew's eyes remained on Pearl, on her soft, blonde-grey hair, on the laugh lines at the corners of her eyes. He could see her teeth beneath her smile: the front tooth had a small chip in it, the only imperfection behind her soft, thin lips. He chuckled to himself, and out of the corner of his eye, the Wildering People's fire leapt again, flames burning a bright orange. Pearl always smiled with her teeth showing, even if she was alone with her own thoughts, which had always made Andrew grin when he looked up from weeding or mowing the lawn and saw her, sitting on the porch with a book, or reclining in the hammock as she was now, eyes closed, resting. Anybody else would have thought she was insane, or having a really good dream, but Andrew knew that that was just Pearl. Always joyful, no matter what the world thought. And if he ever snuck up on her during one of these moments, Andrew would reach down and tap her chipped tooth, startling her and making her laugh a loud, honking laugh until she collapsed into wheezes. "Pearl Goose," he'd call her then, and she would shove him, and in fake anger, reprimand him for disturbing the peace.

"That's beautiful," said Sam, and Andrew's gaze jerked back down from the orb—he hadn't realized he'd spoken aloud.

"Do you talk about Pearl often?" asked another elder, one with a wine-colored shawl. His voice was deep, reverberating in Andrew's ribcage.

Andrew shook his head.

"Not in twenty-five years," piped in Mac. Andrew made a noise, but Mac was right. He couldn't remember the last time he'd said her name out loud to anyone else. He couldn't remember the last time he had mentioned her things, or looked through that packed closet in the entryway, or done anything other than try to exist without her.

Sam and the other elders nodded thoughtfully. "Thank you, Tacito," said Sam, his eyes brighter than the flames next to him. "For sharing a story with us."

"It was hardly a story," said Andrew before he could stop himself. "Just a tiny memory." He looked down at his hands, suddenly embarrassed to be in the presence of these men, with their multi-colored shawls, gentle voices, and weighted words. He felt insignificant. Pearl was his wife, but these men didn't know her. What was the point of sharing her now?

"Perhaps," said Sam, head bent, ruffling through a pocket in his shawl. "In your vault of Pearl stories, it was only a small one. But—" His fingers clasped something, and he withdrew his hand from his pocket. Between his thumb and index finger was a piece of paper with writing on it. He raised his hand, and the firelight illuminated black, scrawled ink. Andrew couldn't make out the words, but before he could ask, Sam tossed the scrap of paper into the flames. There was a pop, and the fire burned an icy blue. As the flames licked the starry sky, a new sound was carried on the smoke and danced under the tree branches overhead—the sound of a flock of geese honking, dissolving into a woman's gasping laughter.

Andrew's heart lurched. He hadn't heard that sound in over twenty-five years. "Pearl," he whispered, whipping his head around. But instead of seeing his wife, there were only the village children and clusters of Wildering adults. They had all stopped too, looking up towards the sound. The children playing the game like hacky-sack let the ball drop mid-toss, craning their necks to the stars.

One of them, a small boy with bright red hair, closed his eyes and smiled wide, revealing gap teeth. A small sound escaped him, a hiccup of a laugh. Soon, the other children followed suit, their gaze still skyward, mouths laughing in unison with the sound of geese above them. As the laughter faded, the fire returned to orange, and the children picked up their ball, jostling each other with renewed energy. But the little red-headed boy turned and looked at Andrew, and he smiled.

"What was that?" asked Andrew, looking at Mac, who only sat, hands folded on his lap, nodding, as if he himself had just shared in some profound secret.

Sam answered him, bending forward so that his long grey hair brushed his knees. "Stories can be beautiful things, Tacito, when we choose to share them. They're universal—many of the messages behind them, and not to be guarded with lock and key. For us, they are life—the good, the bad, the joy, the pain—and we keep them together. You've added to our collection, to our understanding of the world. You've allowed us a moment to consider joy, and laughter, and peace. To slow down and remember our own stories and those same moments within them. To process them differently, because you were willing to process your own."

Andrew didn't know what to say, but he looked over Sam's shoulder at the little red-headed boy, who was now leaping at the other children, laughing maniacally as he tried to grab the hacky-sack ball. Nearby, adults who noticed began to chuckle, their old eyes assuming a younger, more vibrant light as they shared in his joy.

"Pearl was joy," he said softly.

Sam shook his head. "Pearl *is* joy," he said. "And we are *honored* that you shared her with us."

Mac put a hand around Andrew's shoulders—they were shaking. Soft sobs welled in Andrew's throat, but they weren't like before, on the top of the Forgetting Mountain. These were fuller, not so raw and desperate, but imbued with something else—*this* was joy, perhaps, the same joy that radiated through the fire and in the smoke above the village people's heads and in a small children's game behind them.

"Tacito," whispered Mac. "It's time to go."

Andrew nodded, but he didn't move. He wasn't sure he wanted to—he wasn't sure he wanted to leave this place, or this feeling.

"Don't worry," said Sam, sitting back up and folding his hands in his lap. "You're always welcome back here. Macario knows the way." He nodded at Mac, whose eyes blazed in the light of the fire, so much so that, once again, Andrew had to look away.

"And Tacito," continued Sam, as the other elders turned back to the fire and their conversation. "If we don't see you again, remember this: You are a storyteller too. Your words matter—look at how they matter, when you choose to share them." He gestured to the community around him, to the children and the adults and the elders who were laughing and giggling together more than ever, to the fire that spit and crackled even brighter than before.

A small smile formed on Andrew's lips, and his eyes brimmed again. "That wasn't me. That was all Pearl."

"Perhaps," said Sam over his shoulder as he turned back towards the fire and the other elders. "But you brought her here."

***

He still stumbled over roots and rocks, but the Storytellers had revitalized him so much that he did not notice, not even when Mac had to turn around and actually pick him up off of the forest floor because he had got his boot caught in a small, unseen stump in the middle of the path. He could still hear the laughter of the village people, see the flaming hair of the young boy with the gap-toothed smile, and feel the warmth of Sam's touch as he pointed to the glowing orb above Andrew's head.

The orbs. Stories. Pearl. Stories of Pearl. Andrew wanted nothing more than to live inside the orb that had shimmered above his head, sit in that very hammock with his wife, and hold her. Just one more time. *Words resurrect the dead*, Sam had said. But the mountains had called him for a reason, Mac had said, and Andrew wanted to believe it. He wanted to believe that Pearl was here, and that he would find her. Certainly at the top of this mountain, this mountain with the village at the bottom—the village that had allowed him to see his wife again, even in an orb, and feel joy for the first time in decades. This was what revitalized him now—he was sure she was here. If Pearl had journeyed to this. . . world, or Death, or whatever it was, and she had come across the Wildering People, she wouldn't have strayed far. Not with the promise of stories and community and laughter sitting right there.

"Come on, Tacito," grunted Mac, heaving himself over a large boulder. "We're almost there."

"To the top?" panted Andrew, but he was so excited at the prospect of finding Pearl soon that he leapt over the rock with the agility and strength of a much younger man.

Mac, however, shook his head. "The top is not always the peak of the journey, Tacito."

Andrew wasn't bothered by Mac's cryptic words. Pearl was *here*. The joy that had filled his heart and mind by the Storytellers' bonfire was only growing more and more the higher they climbed. His Pearl was *here*. He could feel it, the reality of it, a journey ending, surging through every part of him.

"Pearl," he whispered, and her name on his lips made him smile.

They battled thick underbrush and shoved aside evergreen branches. Andrew stepped past Mac, energy welling up inside him, his heart pounding, and he began to run, ignoring the scratches of the branches through his already-torn corduroys.

"Tacito!" Mac called. But Andrew paid him no attention. He was panting heavily now, but when he looked up, he was sure the orb was still above his head—this time, Pearl was riding her favorite horse, Happy-Go-Lucky, through the fields by their little house while Andrew looked on from the porch, sipping his morning coffee. It was in the early years of their marriage, right when they'd bought the property, and her hair was more golden than ever, a sharp contrast to her horse's dark mane. In the image, Pearl laughed inaudibly as Happy-Go-Lucky broke into a gallop.

In the woods now, Andrew pretended he was riding next to

her, charging through the evergreen branches as if they did not exist. He did not know where Mac was, but still he ran, sharply uphill now, and there was a clearing ahead. Blue sky poked through the trees with no other rock in sight. If he could get to it, there might be a vantage point. . . maybe he'd spot Pearl from there?

Twenty yards away now—

She'd loved bouldering at the base of the mountains across the river back home, when she could find rocks sturdy enough, and with enough handholds. . . perhaps she'd be bouldering here, somewhere?

Ten yards—

He felt like he could run forever if that meant finally finding his wife, and he would, too. *Call to me, mountains! Tell me where she is! I'm here!* Adrenaline coursed through his veins, and the orb above his head swelled, making his hair grow hot. Andrew opened his mouth as he ran, closing the last feet between himself and the clearing in the trees—

"Pearl!" he shouted, hearing the laughter in his own voice. "I'm coming, Pearl!"

He flung his body forward. . . into open space. The ground disappeared beneath his feet, and Andrew looked down, eyes transfixed on the great gully below, and the surging river that plowed a path through it. His heart dropped, and a cry rose in his throat. But, before he could scream, a hand wrapped around his wrist, yanking Andrew backward. His feet tripped over solid earth, and he hit the ground hard, knocking the wind out of his chest.

Next to him at the edge of the ridge, Mac was panting too—the first sign of fatigue that Andrew had seen since meeting him what had to be weeks before.

"Don't. . . do. . . that," gasped Mac, staring at the cerulean sky above them, chest heaving.

Andrew coughed and sucked in a deep breath, wheezing. "I—I'm sorry. Thank. . . thank you," he managed.

Mac grunted in response. "Boy. If that's what one story does to you, Tacito, I can't imagine what will happen when you go back and choose to share more."

Andrew's head swung sideways. "Go back?" he asked. "Go back where?"

But Mac was standing now, staring out over the ridge, eyes locked on a towering purple-grey mountain across the distance the gully created. The nearest rock of this new mountain had to be a quarter-mile away, but as he shifted his weight, pulling himself up so he was reclining on one elbow, Andrew thought he could see the figure of a person against the dull rock. He scrambled to his feet.

"Pearl?" he said wildly, but Mac was already shaking his head. He was breathing normally now, but Andrew's heart still beat faster than normal. He still felt it—the bubbling, softly prickling sensation in his chest that had burst forth from recalling each of the past moments with Pearl. He looked up. The orb was gone, the image of Pearl disintegrated somewhere, but the feeling remained, if not a little muted after having been snatched out of thin air and saved from certain death.

"This is what I wanted to show you," said Mac, gesturing across the gully towards the figure on the mountain.

Andrew hoisted himself to his feet and stood next to Mac, squinting across the gap. Flecks the size of the man's head were falling from the mountain—rocks, breaking off from the mountain face itself.

"Listen," Mac whispered.

Andrew craned his neck forward, and, as his vision came into focus, he heard something, too: a long, loud wail. The man was howling, and as Andrew watched, he drew his leg backwards and swung it forward, striking the rock, pieces of which broke off and crumbled, falling into the gully below. As it happened, the whole mountain seemed to shudder.

"What's going on?" Andrew murmured, and as he continued to watch the man, the joy in his chest faded. Now he felt something else—something like pity.

"You've met the Valley Girl, the Forgetting Mountain, and the Wildering People," said Mac, turning to look at Andrew. His eyes were deep, searching, wise. "You've seen and known what each does for its inhabitants, or those that venture to them. This—" He pointed across the gully. "This is the Altruist."

"That man?" asked Andrew.

Mac shook his head. "The mountain. He does something else entirely."

Andrew looked at the mountain. At first glance, it looked like any other mountain, which was to say, inanimate. But, as Andrew had seen with the Forgetting Mountain, first appearances here were not always what they seemed. He took a deep breath and scanned the mountain again.

As the man on the ridge continued to kick and punch the mountain, wailing and crying, Andrew watched the rock face around him and listened to the sounds that surrounded it, beyond the howls and screams of the man. When the man punched, rocks fell, and the rest of the mountain shuddered. Then the side of the mountain visible to Mac and Andrew rippled, almost as if it were bending over in pain. Then, the rippling stopped, and the mountain straightened up, just in time for another one of the man's blows.

"But. . ." Andrew fumbled for words. "He's hurting it. . . er, him! This. . . destruction. . . it's not helping!"

Mac glanced at him. "Isn't it?" he said quietly.

Andrew gazed out over the gully again. The man punched the mountain again, tearing rocks from its face and hurling them into the ravine. He kicked and scraped the boulders at ground level and pounded the rocks at eye level. Each time, the mountain shuddered, and each time, the man howled louder. But, with every blow, Andrew noticed, the man's arms and legs grew more fatigued, moving slower and slower, blows softening and lessening as he wore himself out. Eventually, the mountain rippled one last time, and the man collapsed, letting out one last howl before he turned towards the rock and curled up against it, chest rising and falling shakily several times before it, too, slowed, until the man was breathing normally, fast asleep against the body of the mountain.

Mac turned to look at Andrew, and Andrew was surprised to see the other man's normally bright eyes duller now, holding a mixture of pity, pain, and yet, somehow, a spark of hope. "This man," said Mac, his voice sounding much older again, "lives with the Wildering People, but he comes here to the Altruist every now and again. He lost his brother in a skiing accident long ago. He blames the mountain—not this one, but others like it, and so, in this place, he spends some time here, slowly destroying the side of the mountain. And the Altruist. . . he takes it. He allows himself to be hurled off into the abyss, or against other parts of himself, every single day, by this man and by others like him, all for their sake. Because, at the end of the day, this man collapses and sobs into the rocks, overcome with what he sees as the futility of his actions to assuage insurmountable grief. And the Altruist comes around him then, to comfort him until the next sunrise, when the pain and anger returns."

Indeed, as Andrew looked across the gap again, he saw the mountain curl towards the sleeping man, trees reaching towards him, rocks softening beneath him, creating something like a massive embrace.

"This man's outlet for pain and sorrow, when it comes," said Mac, his voice low, "is destruction. If the man did not destroy the mountain, he would destroy himself. The Altruist allows himself to be destroyed, so that this man is not."

Andrew said nothing, but his heart filled with pity for both the man on the mountain and the mountain itself. And yet, as the sun sunk closer to the horizon, he couldn't help but notice the man's softened facial features, and the way he snuggled closer to the mountain that wrapped around him, the same mountain that only recently had silently taken his blows.

"Do not be ashamed of the sorrowful times, Tacito," said Mac, eyes burning again. "The Wildering People and their stories—they are both joy and sorrow. Sorrow and joy exist together in grief. They always have, and they always will, just as there cannot be dawn without dusk. Rejoice in the dawn, and take heart in the dusk, because dawn is coming. That is all we can do in this world."

Andrew tore his eyes away from the Altruist. "What do I do, Mac?" he whispered.

The other man's hearty chuckle rocked the trees beside them, and the familiar, down-to-earth Mac was back. "Well, if that ain't a loaded question," he said. "As for you, Tacito, what do you want to do?" He gestured across the ravine to the sleeping man. "Throw rocks?" He pointed to the east, where, in the distance, the Great River glistened and green fields swayed. "Or sit in the Valley for a while?"

At his question, Andrew's shoulders sunk. He had found a spurt of energy after visiting the Wildering People, and it had almost killed him. Now, sitting on this ridge, he realized that he had not slept in what felt like days. Since he had first left his house, he had floated down a river, walked miles in the woods, met Mac, journeyed up three different mountains, and so much more, all in an effort to find his wife. To find his Pearl. But, now, sitting there, watching the Altruist wrap around this man, this man who exhausted himself day after day, in anger, pain, sorrow, and—Andrew realized with a pang in his heart—isolation, he couldn't help but see himself in that previously destructive man, not as he was in his past life back home, but here in this world *now*—if he wasn't careful—forever running and searching for something that might not be found, at least not in the way he'd anticipated.

Mac put a hand on his shoulder. "Do you understand now, Tacito, what this world is?"

Andrew looked at his friend, at his bright, burning eyes, and instead of blinking, Andrew stared back. Images danced in Mac's eyes—the Valley Girl, sacrificially parting rushing waters to provide rest; the Forgetting People, trapped forever in their own desire to avoid pain and reality; the Wildering People, sharing stories that, in some form, brought memories to life; the Altruist, forever allowing itself to absorb the pain and sorrow of those that needed release. And, woven throughout each of these personalities and places, threads of a thousand individual journeys—Mac's Julia jumping rope, Samson's Boulder home erupting in flames, the man whose brother had died in a skiing accident, and of course, Andrew's own Pearl, relaxing in a hammock one day and pinned to a hospital bed the next. And, as Mac had said, there was also pain and joy, forever pulsing between the threads, each inextricable from the other, without beginning and without end.

"Healing," said Andrew, his own voice sounding as if it were coming from somewhere other than his throat, like an echo deep inside him. "This world is for healing."

Mac's eyes glowed brighter, and this time, he was the one to blink; when he opened them again, they were a deep green. "Yes," he said. "Yes."

Andrew closed his eyes, sitting back and looking out at the sunset, which had faded from red to a pinkish-golden, much like the last sunset he had seen from where he'd stood in his own fields, grasses tickling his ankles, old corduroy making his legs itch.

Mac nudged him. "What do you reckon, my friend? Where will you find your Pearl?"

Andrew looked to the east, where the Great River was being dammed by a gentle girl with long, blonde hair and swirling black skirts. *There is good in powerful grief, in a course directed.* In balance, the Valley Girl had meant. In joy and in sorrow, together. Both in going and in resting. In staying and in moving on.

He had been going a long time now without Pearl. A long, long time. He had stayed in the same house for longer than he could really remember—the same, comfortable house with shut-away memories. Keeping stories from even himself. Moving as routine allowed, but never moving on. It was clear to him then, as Andrew sat with his legs dangling off the precipice of a ridge, with the sun cooling against the horizon, next to the closest companion he'd had in years, that it wasn't Pearl who had died twenty-five years ago on that hot July day.

And so, for the first time since he had been without his wife, Andrew acted for himself, to save his own life.

"Let's go to the Valley. I think I'll rest a while."

# Chapter 9

*There is discomfort in reflection, and there is pain in remembering. But here, in the Valley, allow yourself to do both. Remember the good times, and the bad times, and reflect on them. Ponder them. Which moments brought you joy? Which moments, intense sadness? Where is there a connection? (There is always a connection.)*

*Look at the river again, and its banks, and the memories lined up along them. Observe the memories and be reminded of them, but do not be afraid—they cannot hurt you—and do not be ashamed. It is life to remember these things, to remember the pain and joy. Do not forget one over the other. Balance, always there must be balance. And here, in this place of rest, you can find it.*

*Do you remember? That night in the hospital, that last night, when the fireflies flew outside the cracked window, and the breeze ruffled the remaining hairs that peeked out from under her cap? Moonlight shone through the curtains and rested on her face, and she was smiling. You were usually asked to leave by this time, but the nurses and doctors knew that she. . . well, they knew, and so they allowed you to stay.*

*She asked you to sing to her. Do you remember that? Of course you do. . . how could you forget, because your wife knew that you did not sing, and never before had she asked you to. In all the years you were married, she was always the one singing, if she was gardening or hiking or lacing up her boots. Even if she was just relaxing—if she wasn't open-toothed smiling, she was close-lipped humming—making a melody so that you did not have to.*

*But that last night in the hospital, she was very weak, and even opening her mouth to smile was a straining effort. And so, even as she stared at you with fading blue eyes, saying nothing, you knew what she wanted. A song, just one more song, and that you would sing it. You didn't know the words to many songs, and in that moment, staring at your wife's slowly closing lids and the shaky rise-and-fall of her chest, you couldn't remember a single song to save your life.*

*Then, her eyes caught yours again, and she parted her mouth. The moonlight across her forehead glowed all the more, and you knew as she* spoke that it would be the last thing she said to you. Three words, each one ten seconds apart, and difficult: "From. . . your. . . heart."

From your heart. From your heart. All she wanted to hear was whatever your heart could say. And in that moment, you wanted to sob, to howl at the moon, to flip the table next to her bed, so angry were you at the doctors for not doing enough, at her for being sick, at yourself for not being a sufficient presence to make her well. But that's not the heart you wanted to share with your dying wife during her last night on earth, so you didn't. You mustered up the last energy you had, the last words that you, too, would intentionally speak to another human being for a long, long time. Your melody was off, your voice quaked, and your words seemed so unimpressive to you, but when your wife looked at you singing to her—with all the weight, the rest, the love in her eyes—you might have thought it was something otherworldly.

I won't make you remember these words now. You don't have to—this, here, is enough. Piece by piece, remember, and allow these memories to dance across your mind. They don't have to dwell there, but don't push them away. Not here, not in the Valley of Rest. Even remembering that moment now, how do you feel? It is sorrow, but it is joy—your last night with her—and how blessed you were to have that moment. Together. It might have been nothing extraordinary, except she—and you—made it so. And isn't that beautiful?

\*\*\*

Andrew opened his eyes to a blue sky, and he took a deep breath. His hands were pressed flat at his sides, palms cool against the lush, green grass. Next to him, Mac breathed evenly, his own eyes closed, and Andrew didn't have to wonder whom he was thinking about as the two of them rested and reflected in the Valley.

The sun was high in the sky, as it was when they had arrived, and so Andrew did not know how much time had passed. It could have been several hours, or thirty minutes, or a week. Amidst at least a thousand other people—men, women, children, various ages but all here together, lying in the Valley—Andrew had spent the last however long reflecting. He wasn't doing anything special, but as he lay there with his eyes closed, memories came to him—some burst forth and exploded in his mind, while others trickled in on the breeze from the wind across the Great River.

There were some memories that were better than others—he much preferred watching Pearl and himself take a walk in the woods than watching himself sing to her in the hospital—but he didn't push any of them away. They came to him fluidly, one after the other, without distinction or precedence. He simply let them come, whether they erupted in his mind or whether they ebbed and flowed more gently. Some were flashes, and some seemed to last hours: Canning fruit, hiking along the base of the mountains, hunting for embroidery templates in the craft store in town, visits to the hospital, collapsing on the floor at home while baking, the wooden spoon caked in batter clattering to the floor, rushing to the ER—Andrew remembered everything: the good, the bad, and the not-so-delicate.

And he wasn't the only one. All around him as they rested, men, women, and children burst into laughter or dissolved into tears, each one remembering their own sorrows, joys, and intricate mixtures of the two. But all the while, their faces were turned to the Sun, light streaming across their cheeks and sheltering them in warmth. They were supported by the cushion of grass beneath, and reminded, too, by the coursing Great River and the presence of the Valley Girl that there is sacrifice in rest, and that it too is deliberate and not without challenge.

Andrew himself had been learning this as he wrestled with—and rested in—the memories that came to him. It was painful at first, like putting on a pair of shoes he hadn't worn in a long time, but as the soles of his memory were tested, they relaxed, and it became easier to recall the things he had pushed away for so long. There, in the Valley, he was cleaning out the closet of his mind, pulling out dusty boots and dented trekking poles, piecing together a broken cribbage set and taking out, for the first time in twenty-five years, Pearl's old, unplayed mandolin.

The latest memory that had surfaced—the one where he sang to Pearl in a late-night hospital bed—this one was among the most painful. It was the beginning of both of their deaths, but it was also a testament to her life and his love for her. And, for that last reason, he couldn't hate it. It was hard, but he treasured it, and he thought that maybe, if he had to choose one of the memories that had visited him in his time in the Valley thus far, a memory to play over and over in his mind, he would choose this one. Because it was difficult, but it was beautiful, too. His last time with his Pearl. And he wouldn't give that up for anything.

Andrew was not the man who assaulted the Altruist, dwelling deeply in so much pain and hurt and anger that it boiled forth into destruction. And, although there was respite eventually in even this, Andrew had never in his life, before Pearl or after Pearl, allowed such raw emotion to rise in him. He had pushed it away. He was more like the Forgetting Man—or he had been, back in his home—believing everything was all right and not wrestling with the memories that offered so much—pain, initially, yes, but also truth and joy and healing.

"I don't want to forget," he said softly, staring up into the sky. Nearby him, there was a rustle as the Valley Girl's skirts spread, just barely catching and stilling a renegade rapid before it broke past her and into the calming waters that spread past the Valley and into the forest beyond.

*Balance*, Andrew thought to himself. *Balance*. Neither the Forgetting Man nor the Altruist's companion offered complete wholeness. "Moving on" did not mean forgetting the past, or himself, and yet, it did not mean dwelling in it, either, allowing emotions—nostalgia, anger, grief—to consume him. In a compromise of the two, there was further truth: "moving on," Andrew thought to himself, did not have to mean that he was leaving something behind.

"Mac," he said suddenly, turning his face from the Sun and looking over at his friend. "You said once that people journey here for a while and then decide to move on, or they decide to stay and move on."

"Mmmm," said Mac, his eyes still closed.

"Well, I asked you if you had moved on, and you said 'yes, I think so.'"

"Mmmm."

"But," pressed Andrew. "Why are you still here?"

Mac opened one eye, and then he closed it again. "Because it's good to rest. In the Valley."

Andrew made a noise. "Yes, but you have before already, haven't you? And you said that after people have rested awhile, they 'move on.'"

Mac didn't answer.

"And," said Andrew, feeling more annoying by the second, "you said you thought about staying with the Wildering People, but you didn't. You can 'stay' and 'move on' at the same time, but you chose not to stay with them. Why?"

Finally, Mac made a small noise—it might have been a chuckle—and rolled over on his side. "Tacito," he said, but he was smiling. "You listen well. Did you know that? Yes."

"Why are you here, Mac?"

Mac sat up suddenly, his face obscuring the Sun, but Andrew still had to shield his eyes—his friend's head blazed equally bright.

"Do you not yet know, Tacito, why I am here?" asked Mac, and his voice echoed across the grass. Even so, the others in the Valley didn't seem to mind. Only the Valley Girl looked up from the water in which she sat, and catching Andrew's eye, she smiled softly.

"No," whispered Andrew. "I—I'm not sure I do, my friend."

Mac grinned. "'My friend,'" he said. "I like that." His eyes, still a deep, mossy green, made Andrew dizzy. He blinked.

"I am here to be Macario," said Mac, and he sounded a thousand years old again. "A blessing."

"You have been," said Andrew quietly. "More than you know."

Mac bowed his head. "That means a great deal to me, Tacito. Thank you. But," he added, "there is something you do not know."

Andrew sat up. "What's that?" he asked, watching his friend's hands twist in his lap. For the first time since Andrew had met him, Mac looked almost nervous. Beside them, the Great River surged, and a soft sigh blew across the water—the Valley Girl's head was bent, her blonde hair dipping further into the water as she arched her back to block the unfeeling current behind her.

"Andrew," said Mac, and the other man flinched at the use of his real name. "I am the one who called you here."

It was silent for a moment. The grasses swayed, but the water was quiet, and the wind was still, and the only sound that Andrew could hear was his own heart in his chest.

"What?" he asked. "You—*you* called me?" His voice was hoarse.

"Yes," said Mac, looking down at his hands. "I—I needed you to come. So, I asked the mountains to call you." He glanced up into the distance, and Andrew followed his gaze—across the Valley, in the hazy distance, the towering peaks of the Third Mountains seemed to rumble.

"The Third Mountains?" asked Andrew, and his heartbeat rose into his ears.

Mac nodded. "They agreed, because they knew that we could help each other."

Andrew's skin prickled. Something seemed amiss. He let the words tumble from his mouth: "Me, help you? How? I haven't done anything."

Mac looked at him then, and he smiled slightly. "Perhaps you don't see how yet, but I promise you, Tacito, you have. You have helped me, and you will. And now, I can go home again."

"What?" Andrew said wildly. "Go 'home?' Back to the Third Mountains? But, Mac, does that mean that you're—" He couldn't finish his thought.

But Mac only smiled. "Don't worry about the Third Mountains, Tacito. They called you in truth, and they knew what they were doing. This journey was yours, Tacito, for *you* alone. I can only hope it has blessed you as it has blessed me."

"Mac, I. . . but," sputtered Andrew, "I never found Pearl!"

Mac raised his eyebrows. "Didn't you?"

Andrew collapsed back into the grass, but his mind was racing, and rest seemed impossible now. Mac seemed to believe that he had found Pearl, but Andrew didn't understand. His wife was still gone—at least, after all this, he wasn't sure that she was *here*, like he'd originally thought and hoped. In his mind once more, Andrew saw the snowy peaks of the Third Mountains.

"She's there, isn't she?" he whispered.

Mac put a hand on Andrew's shoulder. "Partly, yes, Tacito. In some form. But do you remember the last thing Sam said?"

Andrew wracked his brain, and the image of the tall, long-bearded man in a brown cloak swam into his mind. Against the popping fire, Sam's last words reverberated in the forefront of his memory: *You brought her here,* Sam had said. After he, Andrew, had shared a small story, one filled with joy and tinged with the sorrow that comes from a treasure being categorized as "past," Sam had thanked him. For sharing that joy, for sharing Pearl. The fire had burned blue, and the children had played more fervently, and the community had laughed louder, and the orb above Andrew's head had glowed brighter. Even as he'd left, Sam had thanked him. *You brought her here.*

And, in that moment, the weight of Sam's words, and the truth that they held, settled in Andrew's heart. This whole time—climbing mountains, floating in rivers, resting in Valleys—Andrew hadn't been searching for Pearl. He had been *unearthing* her, all within the fantastic journey of searching for himself. And in finding himself, Andrew had retrieved his Pearl, lost somewhere deep inside him in memories and stories—a buried treasure, only needing to be spoken back to life. *Words resurrect.*

His eyes were hot and wet, and keeping one hand on his heart, Andrew reached up with the other one to dry his tears. But they kept coming, and pressing his face to the Sun once more, Andrew let them come.

"Tacito," whispered Mac, his hand still on Andrew's shoulder. "It is time for me to go."

"Go where?" asked Andrew, opening his eyes. Mac swam in front of him, the outline of his body made blurry by the tears.

Mac gestured to the Third Mountains.

"But. . ." Andrew took a deep breath. "What about me?"

Mac smiled. "That's for you to decide."

Andrew stared at the horizon beyond the Valley. He wanted so desperately to go with Mac, to find Pearl in bodily form. But something tugged at him, and he knew he could not. Not yet. What, then? Back to the Wildering People, to the last place he remembered being submerged in deep, deep joy, and the first place in twenty-five years he had encountered Pearl, raw as it had been? His chest flooded with warmth. But he had found her again, in the stories that pulsed in his memory and in his heart. He had those, always, the Wildering People had said, because he was one, too—a storyteller. His words mattered, Sam had said, when he chose to share them.

Should he share them? With whom? Next to him, Mac's eyes glowed a brighter green.

"I have to go back home," said Andrew quietly.

Mac's smile was dazzling. "If you say so, Tacito." He stood up suddenly, and Andrew scrambled to his feet.

"Well, then," said Mac.

"Well, then," repeated Andrew, looking at his friend. "I. . ." In that moment, words seemed insufficient. "I. . . I hope you find Julia."

Mac closed his eyes and nodded once. "I have, Tacito. I have." He looked again at the Third Mountains.

"Oh," said Andrew, following Mac's gaze. "Yes. I suppose so. Well, then."

Mac only smiled.

A lump rose in Andrew's throat, and he hastily wiped his hand on his now heavily worn corduroy pants. Even in the days when he had interacted with people in any form, he had never been one for goodbyes. "Er. . ." He cleared his throat and tried again. "When will I. . . when will I see you again?"

Mac's grin grew wider. "Soon, I'm sure."

Andrew nodded. "OK. Do you think. . . well, do you think you'll. . . call me again?" He shielded his eyes against his friend's ever-stretching smile.

"No," said Mac, and Andrew's heart dropped. "But someone else will, Tacito. In time. And that will be the last."

"OK."

Mac reached out then, and, clapping one tan, weathered hand on Andrew's shoulder, pulled him into a hug. A breeze blew off the waves on the Great River, but Andrew felt warm. He closed his eyes and took a deep breath. The Valley smelled of goldenrod, and if he squinted, he might have thought these long, swaying grasses were home to his own fields, his own garden, his own house. It would hurt to go back, but in his mind, the house wasn't burning anymore. Perhaps it was ash now, having slowly crumbled in the flames that had licked at its corners as it burned in Andrew's mind, but surely it was at peace now, in whatever state it was in. He had to go see.

Mac pulled away then, and he held Andrew at arm's length, regarding him deeply. Andrew stared back, refusing to blink, even as Mac's eyes went from deep green to light yellow to brighter than the Sun itself. . .

"Who *are* you, Mac?" Andrew asked, his voice a whisper, the question pouring from him like water from the lip of a cascade's ridge.

"I am Macario, here to be a—"

"Blessing," Andrew finished for him, but he wasn't upset.

Mac smiled again—if it were possible, even wider—and his whole face was now aglow. Andrew's eyes burned and watered, and as much as he tried, he could not keep them open. He squeezed them shut, but the burning spread from behind his irises, down his neck and to his arms, where Mac's fingerprints were surely burning holes in his shirt, ten little hot pads scorching his skin—until quite suddenly, they were not.

Andrew opened his eyes again. Before him, the grasses still swayed, and the river still rumbled, and the people around him still rested, their faces serene in the midday sun. Mac, however, was nowhere in sight. In the distance, though, over the top of the Third Mountains, Andrew was sure he could see a sunbeam—a pillar of light jetting from a break in the clouds and down over the first of the great peaks, making a hole in the haze and landing somewhere beyond the horizon. And, over the faintest of breezes, there danced the sound of a young girl's bell-like laughter.

Ignoring the yawning hole in his chest, Andrew turned to the Great River, his eyes drifting over its whitewater and to where the Valley Girl knelt, skirt sprawled and hair dragging in the slowing current. He was unsurprised to find her looking at him.

"How do I get home?" he asked her simply, and even as her hands lifted and parted the gently swirling water in front of her, even as her voice spoke in his mind, Andrew found that his feet were already moving towards the banks with quiet certainty, carrying him exactly where he needed to go.

*Get in the river. The river is safe.*

# Chapter 10

The bucket in his hands was heavier than Andrew expected. It knocked into his knees as he walked, and as he hoisted it into his arms to instead support it from the bottom, some of the sap sloshed up the bucket's side and onto the hand that gripped its handle.

"Oh boy," he muttered as he bent and straightened his fingers. They felt tacky already.

Next to him, Ernest Endelway chuckled. "Don't worry 'bout it," he said in a soft voice that was once again beginning to be familiar. "I lose about twenty percent of what these trees give up through transport each year. . . and I still end up with more syrup than I know what to do with."

Andrew nodded, stabilizing the five-gallon sap bucket under his chin while he positioned his hands once again at its base. "I guess gardening and canning doesn't exactly build up your strength," he said, and Ernest chuckled again.

"Maybe not," he said, "but you're still truckin' through these woods like you've been truckin' through them your entire life."

It was true. As the two men walked through Ernest Endelway's "back forty"—the endless forest behind his and Suzanne's country home—Andrew found himself gliding over tree roots, ducking under low-hanging branches with ease, and effortlessly maneuvering past hidden stumps and turned-up rocks. Ernest wasn't slow either, but there was something about the way Andrew moved—his speed, precision, spatial awareness—that seemed, well, otherworldly.

"Practice, I guess," said Andrew, not really knowing what to say, and Ernest, to his credit, didn't pry.

It had been several months since Andrew had left the Valley of Rest and stepped into the Great River that he knew would take him home. Several months since he had watched the Forgetting Man disappear, said goodbye to the Wildering People, watched the Altruist work his healing work, witnessed the sunbeam that was Mac highlight the summit of the highest peak in the Third Mountains.

Several months since he had woken up just past the fence of his own quiet fields, stepped back into its boundaries, and set off for the little house that waited atop the hill: still, peaceful, unburned. Like he had never left.

All things considered, a very large part of him wanted to dismiss it all—climbing the mountains, resting in the Valley, and everything in between—as some wild, fantastical dream. He had simply drifted off while watching a particularly artistic sunset, and he had awoken the next day, in his same field, looking out over the mountains that he had only imagined had called to him.

But he couldn't. He couldn't bring himself to believe that it all had not been real. In his mind, even months later, while he was weeding, or cooking, or simply walking through the fields by his house, Mac's drawl drifted suddenly into a deep, echoey, timeless wisdom; the Valley Girl's black skirts spread in the coursing, callous river; the laughter and revelry of the Wildering People danced into his ears and through the pictures in his mind as vibrantly as they had when he had been there in person. Because he *had* been there in person. . . hadn't he?

More than anything else, it was the way Andrew *felt* that convinced him his journey had been more than a figment of his imagination, or some strange, elliptical dream. Because, upon waking up in his field, with the looming grey mountains across the steadily flowing river down below, Andrew had felt a thousand things—confusion, joy, wonder, peace—but there was one thing he did not feel: complacency. His house was still standing, but it had been burning before—he was sure of it. The closet in the entryway had spilled a thousand memories, and back in the Valley, he had picked them up, one by one, until they were uncluttered again and visible—back on the shelves but with the door open, so that anyone who might enter could see them. He could not pretend that—in this world now—he could shove them away, and he realized, as he stared unblinking at the cloudless, purple-blue sky above, that he did not want to.

When he had first stepped back into his cabin, he went to the windows, untying the cotton-blue curtains that had been pinned back for the past couple of decades. They were wrinkled at first, and he imagined them protesting in the breeze after being restrained for so long, but as the weeks passed, their wrinkles softened, and they soon floated harmoniously with the brisk spring wind that wafted through the windows. Then, he had gone through that entryway closet for real, taking out Pearl's mandolin, her trekking poles, a thousand board games with their pieces scattered. . . and he rifled through all of it, making two piles. One of the closet-boxes he put back in the closet, which freed up many shelves for some of the new gear he had purchased—new hiking boots, new trekking poles—because he wanted to start hiking again, regularly. The other box he took to town the next day, knocking on the door of Roger's Thrift—and, much to the owner's surprise, donated the entirety of its compartments. He also went to the Food 'N Stuff and bought a large bag of horse feed after asking Fran, the cashier (and resident equestrian) if she knew of anybody in town looking to sell a horse.

"It's Andrew, Pearl's husband," he'd clarified when she'd given him a questioning look. Her face had lit up behind her oversized spectacles, her flyaway grey hair almost quivering with shock and excitement, and she'd sprung around from behind the counter to crush his lungs in a massive—even for her stature—hug.

Over the next few months, Andrew had visited the other shops in town, and every now and then, even stopped in at Pearl's church events. After twenty-five years, a lot had changed, but then again, much had not—the town was still the small, familial place he had remembered it being. Though he still wasn't one to jump at community fundraisers or spend more than an hour at the local watering hole once every two weeks, Andrew did, for the first time since Pearl's death, make an effort to be part of the community. He sold canned preserves—apples and peaches, mostly—at the farmers' market every Friday, each mason jar wrapped in a hastily scrawled label: Pearl's Preserves. It wasn't glamorous, but as they had been twenty-five years ago—even unnamed—Pearl's Preserves were the best in town, and Andrew's booth sold out each week within the first couple of hours of opening.

It was there at the farmers' market one sunny Friday a couple of months after his "return" that Andrew ran into a petite, energetic woman who—decades later—still had the same spiky, short hair, even if it was grey now instead of jet-black. Her husband stood behind her a few feet, as if to make room for her personality, but he was smiling, too.

"Andrew? Andrew?" Suzanne had shouted, and Ernest had laid a hand on her arm to restrain her from bulldozing through the crowd. She was hunched over and shuffled along instead of the agile bouncing he remembered, but Andrew would have recognized her in a heartbeat.

"Hello, Suzanne. It's been a while. Good to see you," he'd said, and was pleased to find that he meant it.

"'A while'?" she'd echoed, pulling him into a hug. "It's been decades. How *are* you?" she blurted, and then immediately looked up, fear washing over her features. "I mean, I'm sorry, I—"

"I've never been better," Andrew had assured her, putting a hand on her arm. She'd smiled then—a bright, sunny thing—and he'd thought of Pearl.

Since that day, he'd visited the Endelway syrup farm more than a few times, and over the last few weeks, Ernest had begun to show him the specificities of his business—how he tapped trees, the process of collecting, and the storage of sap for the late spring when they could begin to boil it down into syrup. Andrew enjoyed the long walks through the forest with Ernest, collecting sap. As before, when they'd made light conversation during their wives' errands, the two men didn't feel the need to fill every silence with sound. The ferns crunched underfoot, the birds sang in the trees, and the sunlight warmed their faces in the cold spring morning. This, thought Andrew, was simple and good.

Back at the house, Suzanne had made a maple pound cake. As the men took off their boots, she set two plates and a couple of mugs down on the kitchen table before turning back to the counter to prepare her own. Andrew watched her dip a large spoon into a pot on the stovetop and glaze the top of her slice with a thick, maple-syrup-based icing. Turning back to the table, he could see she was biting her lip, as if to inhibit herself from speaking.

"Something on your mind, Suzanne?" asked Andrew, taking a

sip of coffee.

She cast him a furtive look before looking plainly at her husband. Over the rim of the mug to his lips, Ernest only tilted his head and looked down as if to say, *Up to you.*

Suzanne put her fork down. "Andrew," she said, staring at him.

Andrew copied her, resting his fork on his plate. "Suzanne."

"Ernest," said Ernest, and chuckled quietly. Suzanne shot him a look, but her husband only smiled and took another sip of coffee.

Suzanne shifted in her seat to face Andrew. "Andrew," she repeated. "I have a question. . . well, it's more of a favor, actually."

Andrew stiffened. "Mmm. . . OK?" he asked, hoping against hope Suzanne wasn't asking him to volunteer as a caller at the next church auction.

"Well," said Suzanne, knitting her knuckles together above her plate. She looked up again. "I don't know what happened to you a couple of months ago, or why. . . or *how*, I mean—well, *how* you. . . it's like you came back to life, you know?"

Andrew nodded, and though he was still concerned about having to begrudgingly accept some volunteer petition, found himself washed in warmth and appreciation for this bubbly-yet-perceptive woman in front of him.

"It's just. . ." continued Suzanne. She paused, and then she flung her hands down at her lap as the words tumbled forth. "I was hoping you might be able to speak to someone."

Something released from Andrew's chest—he was not being asked to run the church auction—but the ambiguity of Suzanne's request kept him guarded. "Who?" he asked. "About what?"

"Well," said Suzanne, glancing at Ernest. "It's. . . a family friend's relative. We don't know him, really, but he's been having a hard time since. . . well, there was a death in the family about a month ago. And—" Suzanne continued before Andrew could speak, "—it's just that. . . he's responding in a similar way to how *you* did when. . ."

"When Pearl died," prompted Andrew.

Suzanne's shoulders seemed to relax. Her face softened and, when she looked at him, her brown eyes were warm. "Yes," she said.

"When Pearl died."

Andrew picked up his fork again, twirling it in his fingers. He was silent for a moment. Then— "Well, then."

"'Well, then' what?" Suzanne prodded, and Ernest laid a hand on her arm.

Andrew didn't respond right away. He couldn't help his initial gut reaction—fear and, of course, constant, pulsing ribbons of insufficiency. What was he supposed to say? The words that others had spoken to him in the aftermath of Pearl's death—words like *I'm so sorry for your loss*, and *She's in a better place now*, and *Stay strong, it'll all be OK*—were empty and unhelpful. They offered no respite, because they tried to substitute respite for the aching, gaunt pain that, although terrible and awful in the realest sense of the words, was still *necessary*. It *had* been necessary, Andrew knew. Not to be pushed away, but balanced, always balanced. This, too, however, was something learned and not told. In that moment, bathed in the light streaming through the Endelways' kitchen windows, Andrew thought again of Mac. How he had journeyed by Andrew's side, hiking mountains and descending onto ridges and valleys, guiding him every step of the way but never insisting on a perfect path. A true companion. But, even at Andrew's side, Mac could not have led if Andrew had not chosen to follow.

"I can talk to him," said Andrew quietly. "If he's willing to listen."

Suzanne's face lit up, and then she softened again. "That would really be wonderful, Andrew. Thank you. His family lives in a town nearby—he's staying with them, but my friend said they would all come to the Town Nights Festival bonfire this weekend, if you'd be willing to come. . .?"

Andrew grimaced. He looked at Ernest. "Are you going?"

"Of course he's going," said Suzanne, as if it were a ridiculous question. Ernest made a gesture: *Well, there you go.*

Andrew took a deep breath. The Storyteller's words ran through his mind for what seemed like the fiftieth time, though this time, there was a pressing sense to understand and believe the truth of them: *Your words matter, when you choose to share them.*

***

Andrew had not been to a Town Nights Festival bonfire since before Pearl had died. This Friday, there were more people than he remembered there being. Crowds milled throughout the boutique district, which was really just the street adjacent to Main and which had a locally crafted jewelry store, a few small-scale designer shops, and a salon or two. Doors were held open by bricks and music drifted between the shops. The bonfire itself, situated behind the Food 'N Stuff (and strategically close to the river), was at least twenty feet high. A few of the younger men from the town—the designated fire-watchers—sat on piles of logs with buckets of water at their feet. They joked amongst themselves and waved at clusters of women as they passed—women from a few towns over who, though they came to shop the boutiques' sales, usually doubled back to the fire more than a few times to make the men's acquaintance.

Other folks, young and old, sat in lawn chairs at least thirty feet away from the fire, sipping hot cocoa. Children with chocolate-stained lips dashed between the chairs playing tag or snuck down to the river to catch crawfish if they could find them. The sight of men, women, and children milling about or sitting, playing, and laughing. . . it tickled Andrew's memory, and standing on the back porch of the Food 'N Stuff taking it all in, he thought of the Wildering People's village. A soft pain tugged at his heart, and in that moment, he wished that he could go back—he wished that he could sit at Sam's feet and listen to a thousand stories of the Boulder family's generational antics, or understand what had caused the wheelchair-bound Storyteller to lose his legs, to hear about the pain and the healing and the delicately woven journey between the two.

But, even as he wistfully remembered that night, sitting with Mac by the Wildering People's fire, Andrew was still glad. He was glad to watch these people—alive and laughing here, too, in this town. He was glad, even in the background, to be a part of it all.

"Andrew," whispered Suzanne to his left. "That's him, over there, by the fire." She pointed.

Andrew followed her finger. In the midst of the clusters of people, there sat a man in a blue lawn chair, covered in a knitted blanket, set apart from any other group. He was hunched over, facing the flames, and as he reached up to draw back his hood because of the heat, Andrew saw a shimmer of silver hair above the man's lips. Andrew's heart tugged at him. Even from a distance, this man looked familiar, but he couldn't place why.

"I think his family is out shopping," whispered Suzanne. "But they know you're coming. He knows too."

That was a start, Andrew thought. This man was willing to talk to *someone*. Andrew couldn't have said the same thing about himself a month after Pearl had died.

"I'll be around," Suzanne said, touching his arm. Andrew nodded, his hands numb. Whatever Sam had said, he didn't feel that he was in any sort of capacity to provide advice, guidance, or some blathering, random story about his dead wife, a woman that this man did not know. But it did not matter, Sam had said, whether or not people knew Pearl. That wasn't the point of stories, or the reason they spoke healing. In this large group of festival-goers—a couple hundred people laughing and running and chittering on about the minor details of their daily lives—there might be no one who understood this man's pain. The raw, gaping hole that death had left in his chest, a hole that would not be filled no matter what he tried to pour into it—distraction, vices, whatever they were, they were like sand cascading into a bottomless pit. Not even stories could fill that void. But maybe, just maybe, they could begin to coat and soothe the gritty, sandpaper edges.

Andrew walked down the steps of the Food 'N Stuff, hands shaking. *Words resurrect*, he told himself over and over again as he stepped closer to the fire, feeling his skin start to heat and his eyes start to water even within forty feet of the flames. A few feet from the man, he stopped.

The man didn't move. His profile was in shadow, but before Andrew could speak, he heard a voice—old, tired, accented. "You must be Andrew," he said.

Andrew nodded, and then cleared his throat. "Yes." He took

out a blanket from under his arm—one Suzanne had thought to bring—and spread it out upon the ground. He sat, cross-legged, and, shielding his eyes, looked up at the man. "And you are?" he asked, realizing Suzanne, in all her excitement and nervous fretting over the past week—which had done nothing for Andrew's own nerves—had neglected to tell him what this gentleman's name was.

"Ignacio," said the man, and he looked down at Andrew.

Andrew sucked in a breath. This man *did* look familiar. He had silver-white hair, and a large mustache. His eyes were green, a deep green, the same color of the evergreen trees that dotted the shores of the river beyond the fire they now sat by. Now, they were tired and dull, but Andrew found himself imagining them, years—or even weeks—before, and how they must have twinkled.

Ignacio looked away, into the fire. "I don't want to take much of your time," he said, staring at the flames. "I don't even know why I came."

Andrew swallowed. "Did your family make you come?" he heard himself ask.

Ignacio looked at him, and beneath the mustache, his lips twitched into something like a smile. Then, it was gone. "Not exactly," he said.

Andrew waited, but Ignacio was quiet. Then, before Andrew could speak, he continued: "I've been alone for a long time, Andrew. Even before. . ." He sucked in a breath. "Even before the accident. They. . . my family isn't around much, except. . . well, they're gone now." Ignacio stopped then, and his mustache quivered under shaky breaths. He cleared his throat, frowned for a moment, and then nodded. "Yes, well. My sister knows. She knows your friend—the bouncy one. She—ah—"

"Suzanne," Andrew offered.

"—Suzanne," Ignacio nodded. "Suzanne told her that she had a friend who had. . . had lost his wife." He glanced at Andrew. "And, well, that it. . . it almost killed him."

Andrew was quiet.

Ignacio sucked in another rattling breath. "Some days," he said, his voice rough and quiet so that Andrew had to lean in to hear him, "some days, I think that might be OK."

A lump formed in Andrew's throat, and he was conscious of the huddled man next to him, probably his own age but who, in this moment now, appeared a hundred years older.

"But then," said Ignacio, through gritted teeth. He swallowed, and his voice was softer, musing. "I think what a disservice that would be, to them. To live this way."

"Yes," said Andrew quietly. "I understand."

"I know you do," said Ignacio, looking at him then, and in the firelight, his eyes were a golden-green, wide and pleading. His hands, light brown and deeply callused, appeared from under his blanket as he clutched Andrew's arm. Then, looking down at his fingers, Ignacio opened them, released Andrew, and withdrew his hands back under the blanket and to himself.

"Your Pearl. . . she was wonderful, wasn't she?"

Andrew's heart grew warm. "Yes. She was the best person I knew," he said softly.

Ignacio grunted and nodded; his eyes closed. "I bet she was."

Andrew didn't say anything more. It was not the time.

"Suzanne said that you went to the mountains," said Ignacio suddenly.

"I did." Andrew's voice was soft. "They called me."

Ignacio frowned at him. "That's what she said, too. She sounded doubtful, or at least confused."

Andrew said nothing. Beside them, the bonfire crackled and spit as two of the fire-watching men loaded a few more logs at its base.

"*Te creo,*" muttered Ignacio. "I believe you," he said again, more loudly.

Andrew raised his eyebrows. "You do?" he asked.

Ignacio's gaze slid from the fire to Andrew. His green eyes held the faintest of twinkles. "Of course. The mountains called to you like the river calls to me each week. It tells me where the best fish are, it whispers when is best to lay the net, and when is best to take 'er up again. It's been quiet this last month, but I think that's because it wants me to take a break. To go to the forest for a bit, because that's where they would be. It was the forest that told me to come here, anyways."

"Ignacio," said Andrew suddenly. "Whom have you lost?" His question was soft, gentle, patient, but Andrew's heartbeat was loud in his chest. The blood in his ears pounded, and he swallowed to try to push it down, but the more he looked into the soft green eyes before him, the more he was sure. But how? How could it be?

"My son," whispered Ignacio, eyes still locked on Andrew. "And my granddaughter. Last month, in a car accident not too far from here." His eyes welled, and he blinked.

Beyond the bonfire before them, the trees of the forest by the river danced in the evening breeze. A creaking arose from their twisting trunks, and in the branches, the sound of an axe—the solid *thunk* of metal sticking in thick, fissured wood—rang into the night. Though it was dark, the fire was warm, and the light from the flames made the shadows of the forest flicker past the veil of smoke: light moving through trees, the forest bent to its will.

A thousand things flashed through Andrew's mind: a black-and-red flannel darting effortlessly through tight clusters of pines; the tip of a hat over bright, winking green eyes; the image of a red truck habitually tracing the curving white lines of a country road. The sound of bells and singing and dark braids swinging as they bounced under a nylon rope. And always, the sometimes-drawling, sometimes-timeless voice that was as sure as the forest itself:

*Julia's favorite thing was to visit her abuelo. My father. He lived a few towns over, by himself in a little cabin. He fished and sold the fish to the local grocery store every Monday.*

In Andrew's mind, a red truck swerved. Red-and-black flanneled hands overcorrected, and it was dark. And Mac's voice:

*She was eight years old when I lost her.*

Mac had been driving when the truck had crashed. Julia had died. On the mountain with Mac so many months ago, hearing the pain in his voice as he recounted the loss of his daughter, Andrew had understood. His heart had yearned for the very man that sat in front of him now—how this man had to have coped with the loss of his granddaughter; and Andrew had yearned for Mac, too—how he must have grappled with the death of his sweet little girl.

*She was eight years old when I lost her.*

But how old were *you*, Mac? How old were you when your father lost *you*? When neither your daughter nor you arrived for your weekly fish fry? Did you understand the pain he went through—do you understand the pain he goes through now—as he mouns you both?

*I am here to be Macario—a blessing.*

Yes, you were, you were, of course you were. Without you I could not have found Pearl again, I could not have understood the depths and heights of my own loss—the loss of myself and her and the life we had together—I could not begin to gather it to myself, to process it, to set aside what I had to and hold close to what I could . . . none of that would have been possible—none of that would be possible still—if not for you.

*You have helped me,* Mac had said, *and you will.*

"Ignacio," Andrew said, and for a moment, his voice seemed to echo in his ears. "Would you. . . would you tell me about them?"

Ignacio's eyes grew hard for a moment, like moss that had been dried too long in the sun. But then, after regarding Andrew for a moment, the muscles in his face relaxed. "You. . . want to hear about my Macario? And my Julia?"

Andrew swallowed, blinking back his own tears. "Yes," he whispered. "If you'd be willing to share."

Ignacio gave a short, barking laugh. "I didn't talk much 'bout my kids to strangers, even when they were alive."

"We're not strangers," said Andrew gently, and Ignacio smiled.

"No," he said after a moment. "No, I don't guess we are. And you wouldn't be a stranger to Mac, if you'd met him. That's for sure." His eyes grew wistful.

Andrew nodded, a small smile at his lips. "I bet not," he said.

Ignacio grunted and looked into the fire. "Perhaps we could walk in the forest in a bit, or maybe tomorrow. But for now, I think I'll just sit here. If that's OK." He looked at Andrew again. "My sister says that it's not good for me to sit around." He shrugged and stared into the fire. "Then again, she don't much want me truckin' around in the forest either."

Andrew thought for a moment. "Everyone moves on eventually, whether it's here or there," he said. "They search a while, or rest a while, or hike in forests a while, or sit by fires a while, and then they figure they better stop that and move on, or keep doing that and move on."

Ignacio looked at him sideways. "Mmm," he said. "Macario used to say somethin' like that."

The two men were quiet then. In front of them, the fire crackled and spit, and music played from the Main Street district where lanterns were strung and people danced and shopped and ate and sang. Above, the stars were bright, and the Milky Way was visible above the smoke and the treeline—a white, twinkling pathway spilling overhead, past the town and out over the black, silhouetted peaks in the distance.

The egg of that day's sun had long since cracked—and all traces of its golden yolk were gone from the bowl of the horizon before them—but it would be back, Andrew knew. A new day would come, like it always had. The egg would rise from the depths of the earth, perfect and whole and bright, soaking up the dawn of the horizon and transforming it into day. The winds would blow across the long, waving grasses of his field, and Pearl's old, tattered hammock would wave with them. And this time, so would the cotton-blue curtains from springtimes long past, and the tangled tails of a single dappled horse that once again made the grasses of the valley home. It was simple and good, simple and good, unlike he'd ever known.

And beyond his field ran the valley, and the silently flowing river, and beyond even these: solid, towering rock that rose—at the farthest visible regions—into snow-crusted peaks. Sometimes, on a windy day, he would stand just beyond the edge of his crumbling fence, facing them, and feel the wind whip through his clothes. The corduroy pants he still wore from time to time, but now, with a thin piece of flannel sewn to the inside of the cuffs, they didn't itch so much anymore. On the days that he wore them—those windy days— he would stand in the field as he did before, and listen. But the mountains hadn't called to him since. Still, with a craning neck and sensitive ears, sometimes—*sometimes*—he thought he might be picking up something. Not a call like a summons, but something else. A melody, perhaps. The beginnings of a song, surely: one whose soft, yearning tones were last heard in a moonlit hospital room as he looked into the dying eyes of his Pearl. And though, these days, he was the only one standing in the open field, he was not alone. Because there, riding on the wind that blew from the ancient, enduring peaks beyond, there came from the mountains to the man a song—a story—one that they could tell together.

www.ingramcontent.com/pod-product-compliance
Lightning Source LLC
Chambersburg PA
CBHW031240260626

47169CB00007B/2394